# BUSINESS AS USUAL

Business had been booming at Bolt's Bawdy House, especially since young Dan Eperwinkle began playing the piano for the evening crowds. But there was always someone trying to destroy Bolt's success. And tonight it was Bob Steckley.

"Well, lookey here," he blurted. "A sissy piano player! Look at them del-eee-cate hands. I bet they never even stroked a woman's behind!"

Dan, his face turning red with rage, rose from the piano stool. He doubled his fist and landed an upper cut to the drunk's chin. Bolt stepped in, jerked Steckley by the britches, and with one forceful kick, booted him out the door.

"You okay?" Bolt asked Dan.

"My knuckles sting a little," he said, half chuckling.

Wanda, who'd been sitting nearby, watched intently as Dan began to rub his hand. The more she watched, the harder it became to sit still. Finally, she jumped up and ran over to Dan.

"I've got some salts in my room," she purred coaxingly. "Come on, Dan. I'll take care of you." Sliding her arm under Dan's and leading him away, she threw Tolt a haughty look.

He nearly laughed out loud, thinking how tonight Dan would have more than his hand taken care of. . . .

# THE GUNN SERIES BY JORY SHERMAN

**GUNN #1: DAWN OF REVENGE** (590, $1.95)
Accused of killing his wife, William Gunnison changes his name to Gunn and begins his fight for revenge. He'll kill, maim, turn the west blood red—until he finds the men who murdered his wife.

**GUNN #2: MEXICAN SHOWDOWN** (628, $1.95)
When Gunn rode into the town of Cuchillo, he didn't know the rules. But when he walked into Paula's cantina he knew he'd learn them. And he had to learn fast—to catch a ruthless killer who'd murdered a family in cold blood!

**GUNN #3: DEATH'S HEAD TRAIL** (648, $1.95)
When Gunn stops off in Bannack City, he finds plenty of gold, girls and a gunslingin' outlaw. With his hands on his holster and his eyes on the sumptuous Angela Larkin, Gunn goes off hot—on his enemy's trail!

**GUNN #4: BLOOD JUSTICE** (670, $1.95)
Gunn is enticed into playing a round with a ruthless gambling scoundrel. He also plays a round with the scoundrel's estranged wife—and the stakes are on the rise!

**GUNN #5: WINTER HELL** (708, $1.95)
Gunn's journey west arouses more than his suspicion and fear. Especially when he comes across the remains of an Indian massacre—and winds up with a ripe young beauty on his hands . . .

**GUNN #6: DUEL IN PERGATORY** (739, $1.95)
Someone in Oxley's gang is out to get Gunn. That's the only explanation for the sniper on his trail. But Oxley's wife is out to get him too—in a very different way.

**GUNN #7: LAW OF THE ROPE** (766, $1.95)
The sheriff's posse wants to string Gunn up on the spot—for a murder he didn't commit. And the only person who can save him is the one who pointed the finger at him from the start: the victim's young and luscious daughter!

*Available wherever paperbacks are sold, or order direct from the Publisher. Send cover price plus 50¢ per copy for mailing and handling to Zebra Books, 475 Park Avenue South, New York, N.Y. 10016. DO NOT SEND CASH.*

# BOLT #2
### BY CORT MARTIN
## DEAD MAN'S BOUNTY

**ZEBRA BOOKS**

**KENSINGTON PUBLISHING CORP.**

ZEBRA BOOKS

are published by

KENSINGTON PUBLISHING CORP.
475 Park Avenue South
New York, N.Y. 10016

Copyright © 1981 by Cort Martin

All rights reserved. No part of this book may be reproduced in any form or by any means without the prior written consent of the Publisher, excepting brief quotes used in reviews.

Printed in the United States of America

# BOLT #2

## DEAD MAN'S BOUNTY

# CHAPTER ONE

The chair scraped along the hardwood floor as Bolt pushed away from the table. He stood up, hunched his shoulders forward. Threw them back until his elbows almost touched behind his back. He flexed muscles that were beginning to stiffen. It was 3:00 a.m. and Bolt had been at the poker table for almost five hours.

"It's late, gentlemen," he said. "Thank you for the game." He shoveled chips into his hat, smiled at the other players.

The smell of whiskey and perfume, cigar smoke and beer lingered in the air even though the orchestra at the Alamo had stopped playing a couple of hours before and the bar was nearly empty.

As Bolt made his way to the cashier's cage, he was approached by a big, bullnecked man.

"You headin' back to your place?"

"Yeah. Only won four hundred tonight."

"Well, step lightly. There's someone lookin' for ya, and he's got 'bounty hunter' stamped all over his face. He's been around three days now, askin' questions. I hear he likes to work at night, and he's got a couple of flankers with him."

"Know who they are?"

"Yeah," said the man who was named Bull Bob Franklin. "One of 'em's a big German feller, bigger'n me. They call him Ox-Man. Joe, the bartender, said he recognized him. Said he was a bounty hunter with a reputation fer gettin' his man at night. Joe says his name's Herb Packmeyer. I heard the Ox-Man say he'd been talkin' to Judge Wilkins over to Coffeyville."

"Hmm." Bolt paused, thinking. So old man Wilkins was still after his ass. "What about the other two?"

"Aw, one of them's just a kid, a drifter, I reckon. He's tall and scrawny, but those beady eyes of his give 'em a real mean look. They call him Pete. Think his last name's Norton. He doesn't look strong enough to fight his way out of a paper bag, but he talks big. The third feller's not as tall as the other two, but he's got a lot of muscle. Wears dirty clothes and a grimy coonskin cap. And he's packin' a matched set of Peacemakers. They call him Will. Will Atterbury. Name ring a bell?"

"Yeah, the name rings a bell."

Bolt didn't want to tell Bull Bob too much, but, yes, he knew the name. Will Atterbury was a damn Jayhawker. At least he'd been one a couple of months ago. Evidently he'd turned bounty hunter. The sonofabitch! Atterbury was one of those damned Jayhawkers he and Tom had run across over near Baxter Springs. Rode with that asshole Scoggins. Bolt would never forget that day. Scoggins was the first man he'd ever killed.

An involuntary shudder coursed through Bolt's body as he thought about that bloody day. Jayhawkers were bad news, trying to collect money from drovers for bringing their cattle across the boundries. Hell, them Jayhawkers didn't own the territory. They got what they deserved. After Scoggins and two other Jayhawkers bought it, Atterbury was one of those who ran scared and hightailed it for safer grounds. So now that bastard was a bounty hunter, a big brave fuckin' bounty hunter.

"Scum of the earth."

"Huh? Oh yeah. Bounty hunters," said Bull Bob. "Just thought you'd like to know."

"Thanks, Bull Bob. I'll brighten up."

Bolt cashed in his chips, walked out into the dark night and stood there long enough for his eyes to adjust to the blackness. He stood away from the stained glass inset where light poured through. He reached down and loosened his '73 Colt single action in its holster, patted it for reassurance.

Bolt was a tall lanky man. His wide shoulders made him look taller than six feet. His sleek, coal black hair was shoulder length. He had clear blue eyes, aquiline nose, a strong square jaw.

Massive clouds hung in the August sky, hiding the full moon behind their velvety curtains. He made his way slowly in front of a darkened building, glad for the darkness.

The street was quiet, deserted at that late hour. Too quiet. He couldn't make out any movement or odd shapes, but he knew he was being stalked.

He could feel it. His scalp tingled. The hairs on the back of his neck stood out. He took two more steps, stopped. Listened. Seconds ticked by. It seemed like hours.

Another step.

A noise.

A slight scraping noise. A flicker of light seamed the street. Bolt halted in his tracks, peered through the gauze of night. Someone across the street had struck a match. Was that the bounty hunter? One of the three who were after him? He quickly ducked between two buildings and waited, holding his breath.

No. Just a drunk taking a leak. He watched the silhouette of the man stagger on down the street. Bolt let his breath out and wiped his sleeve across his face. He had about a half a mile to walk to his place and so far he had only gone three doors beyond the Alamo.

He darted across a vacant lot, his footsteps pounding in his ears, magnifying in his brain. He made it to the next building where he paused, listening again. Hard.

He took a few more cautious steps. A cat yowled as Bolt stepped on its tail. Bolt froze. Adrenlin dumped into his bloodstream. He didn't move a muscle. The injured cat skittered away, around the building. He waited a long time before he dared to step out again. If anyone was following him, they would know where he was. They'd had their chance to attack him. Yet no one had made a move.

*Maybe Bull Bob was making things up.*

Maybe, hell.

Bull Bob was no jester. He was a hotel clerk and he watched people close. Real close.

If Franklin said someone was hunting him, then someone was.

He inched his way along the few remaining false fronts, hugging their shadows. He knew what lay ahead of him — a huge empty field that offered nothing in the way of cover except some tall grass and a few scattered trees. If he could just get to the stockyards beyond that field, he'd have it made. His place lay just beyond there, down by the railroad tracks.

The moon floated out from behind the clouds, illuminating the landscape. It was like daylight. Bolt tucked into the doorway of the general store. A wooden sign proclaiming Jensen's Mercantile Store rattled on its hinges as a light breeze caught it. Bolt scanned the huge vacant field he knew he had to cross. Tall dark forms sprinkled the landscape. Pine trees, he knew. Would be a good place for an ambush — or a bad place, depending on who was doing what.

Above him, the clouds played tag with the moon, touching it before moving on, eclipsing it briefly. Bolt studied the sky. Only a few small clouds hovered near the planet, but off to the west were massive clouds, suspended like freshly picked cotton. He'd have to wait for complete darkness again before he could make his way across the open space.

He stuck a finger in his mouth, brought it out slick with saliva. He held it up in the night air, felt the backside of his finger begin to cool as the wind touched it. The wind was blowing from the right direction. It wouldn't be too long before the clouds would cover the moon again.

A quarter of a mile ahead, out of earshot, three men huddled behind a clump of pines by the side of the road.

"He's got to come this way," said Ox-Man. "It's the only way back to his place."

"But what if he don't come tonight?" said a nervous Pete Norton.

"He will," said a steely-eyed Will Atterbury.

"Yeah," said Ox-Man, "soon's he's through playin' poker."

"Maybe he'll find himself a woman and spend the night," offered Pete.

"Ain't no glitter gals over to the Alamo," said Will.

"He don't buy his women anyway, I hear," said the big burly man. "Poker's his game. He'll be along. Now, we're goin' ta spread out. I'll stay here behind these trees. Pete, you go up the road aways, take cover behind that pine t'other side of the road." He gestured with a ham-sized fist. "Will, you go back yonder to them other trees, across the road. We'll form kind of a triangle that way. Trap him in the middle. Wait till we got him in between us before we make our move. He's got three pistols aimed at his gut, he'll give up real easy. Don't shoot him. I want that sonofabitch alive!"

"Sure hope it stays bright. Make it easier fer us," mumbled Pete as he headed up the road.

Bolt had a decision to make. The clouds were finally drifting toward the moon and he wouldn't have much time to make his way across the field. The shortest and quicket path would be along the dirt road. But would it be the safest way? Something deep inside him gnawed at his senses, set his nerves jangling. Those damned trees along the road! That's what made him nervous. Too much chance of a trap. If those bastards were really laying for him, like Bull Bob said, that's where they'd be waiting. He could feel it in his bones.

An owl screeched in the distance like a warning bell. He'd take his chances in the field, stay away from the road.

When the clouds covered the moon again, Bolt was ready. He crouched low, his right hand hovering above his holstered pistol, and left the security of the dark buildings. He darted across an open space and reached the tall grasses of the vacant field. He paused and listened. A dog barked somewhere back toward town. He snuck a few more feet, stopped. Nothing. He ran through the grasses, keeping low, until he reached a single tree in the middle of the field. He paused there to catch his breath, stretch his cramped legs. The wind blowing through the leaves sounded like a rushing river.

From his position, Bolt could see the dark outlines of the pines scattered alongside the road. He could detect no movement near the trees. He began to relax. Maybe Bull Bob was wrong, although he had said that Ox-Man and his gang liked to work at night. Only a little farther to go and he'd be at the stockyards. Then, a short walk to his place. He had it made. Almost.

He crouched again, dashed to the stockyards. He reached a small ramshackle building. He eased around the corner of the structure, feeling his way like a blind man, deft fingers against the rough hand-cut lumber. His boots kicked over small rocks. He stumbled over a metal object and the clanging noise shot through the night air like a dinner bell. He leaned over, felt it. A damned bucket. He stood quiet, clinging to the outside of the building, listening with keen ears.

A twig snapped somewhere behind him!

Panic drenched him for a split second. He drew his pistol with his right hand, picked up the bucket with the other. In one smooth motion, he hurled the bucket as far as he could, twirled around, cocked his Colt. Waited. The bucket crashed to the ground forty feet away.

A shot erupted behind him. He heard the spang of the bullet hit the bucket.

He was ready.

He aimed at the orange flame hanging in the darkness, squeezed the trigger. A scream rang out, reverberated through the clear air. Bolt heard the stalker crumple into the tall grass. And then everything was silent.

Deadly silent.

Bolt knew there were two more men out there somewhere, tracking him like an animal. If he could get a couple of those small rocks he had stepped on, that would be all the ammunition he would need for now. He spidered his hand around in the dirt next to the building until he found some loose rocks, picked them up and stuck them in his hip pocket, holstered his pistol. He snuck around to the back of the wooden shack. The roof in the back was very low. With arms extended upward, he jumped high, caught the hand-hewn shingles and pulled himself up with strong muscles. The top part of his torso jackknifed on to the roof and he threw his legs up. He scrambled to the high point of the roof line, drew his pistol again and lay prone. Motionless.

Minutes later he heard heavy footsteps running toward him. He turned his head, strained to separate each individual footfall. He detected two distinct sets of footsteps: one much heavier and closer, snapping twigs and brush with its weight; the other, farther away, but coming up on him faster.

"Pete, that you?" yelled a deep husky voice.

Bolt lured him on. "Yair, over here," Bolt said softly, hoping his voice wouldn't give him away.

"Didya kill him, Pete?" Ox-Man yelled.

"Yeah, I got 'im." Again in a low voice.

Too late, Ox-Man realized his mistake. That wasn't Pete's voice. Nor Will Atterbury's. The clouds were beginning to thin around the moon as Herb Packmeyer came across the bloody body in the tall grass. In the pale glow of the moonlight, he could see that Pete Norton had bought it. Too bad. The kid never really had a chance to grow up. He had talked a good fight, but never made it.

Ox-Man kept low, scanning the landscape for Bolt. He heard footsteps coming up fast behind him. Knew it was Atterbury.

Bolt made his move. Perched on top of the roof, he threw the rocks, arched them high so they would fall to the ground directly below him, next to the building. It worked.

Twin orange flames spurted from the darkness as Herb and Will shot simultaneously at the noise. Bolt fired quickly, first at the spot where one flame had been a second ago, then at the other target. One bullet found its mark as the big Ox-Man fell to the ground, blood gurgling from his throat.

His second shot missed. Another shot rang out. Bolt ducked, felt the bullet whiz over his head. The third man had spotted him.

Bolt crawled to the back side of the building, jumped to the ground, ran around the corner of the structure.

The moon popped out from behind the clouds, briefly lighting the area. Two bloodied bodies lay silvered in the moonlight. Bolt and Atterbury stood thirty feet apart, staring at each other for a split second before the moon tucked back into its hiding place. It was just long enough for Bolt to get a good look at Atterbury. The image burned indelible on his brain. The look on Atterbury's face was one of horror. Terror flashed from his wide pale eyes. His mouth hung open in a silent scream. He raised his gun just as the clouds blotted out the moonlight.

Both men fired at the same time but the bullets missed their marks. Bolt heard Will running through the bushes, fired once more. The quick footsteps got farther and farther away until Atterbury was too far out of range to waste another bullet on him.

Bolt dragged the two bloody bodies into the heavy brush and dumped them. Let someone else take credit for these two.

He headed home, suddenly exhausted. He wouldn't have to worry about Will Atterbury any more tonight. He was running true to form. Splitting for safer grounds once the going got rough. Will wouldn't stalk him again tonight. Not by himself. He didn't have the guts for it. He was just a lousy Jayhawker turned bounty hunter.

Bolt pulled his lean muscular frame to its full height, strolled back to the road that crossed in front of the stockyards. The night sky seemed to close down on him. He could not shake the image of Atterbury's frightened face. It was a face he'd seen before. A face he would not forget now.

It was nearly 4:30 when Bolt reached his place. He went through the back door of the combination hotel, saloon and bawdy house. He walked around through the empty lobby, turned left and headed down the hall to his room in the back. He brought out his key, placed it in the lock and turned it. Instinctively cautious, he opened his door, swinging it wide.

Something moved inside the darkened room. Startled him.

His hand streaked for his gun.

## CHAPTER TWO

"That you, Bolt?" A sleepy voice out of the darkness. A soft, feminine voice.

Just in time. Bolt, his nerves frayed, was slightly trigger happy.

"Were you expectin' someone else?"

A warm glow filled the room as she lit the coal oil lamp next to the bed, turned the wick down.

"No, just you, Bolt." Her laugh was provocative, sensuous. "You must have had good luck at poker tonight."

"I did okay." Bolt smiled at the beautiful woman sitting on his bed, her long legs dangling over the edge. Cassie Owens smiled back. Her long dark hair fell gracefully around smooth bare shoulders. The tops of her creamy white breasts mounded invitingly above the lacey edge of the low-cut nightgown. Her blue eyes sparkled with desire.

"I thought I heard shots. I was worried."

"Nothing to worry about. Now."

"Maybe I shouldn't ask you any more about it."

"Best not to, Cassie."

"I've kept the bed warm for you, Bolt," she husked.

"I hope you kept more than that warm for me, Cassie." His lips curled into an impish grin. He reached over, secured the bolt on the door, then removed his belt and hung his pistol on the bedpost. Began unbuttoning his shirt.

Cassie scooted back over to the middle of the bed, exposing her dark thatch as she moved. The action wasn't wasted on Bolt. He caught a glimpse of her smooth bare thighs and the nest of her honeypot between them. Fire sparked in his loins. He felt the first twinge of desire stir his manhood to life. The sweet fragrance of lavender floated in the air, erasing the stench of death that clung to him.

He sat on the edge of the bed, kissed her tenderly before taking off his boots.

"You smell so sweet, Cassie."

"You want me, Bolt?"

"Yes, I want you. I'm glad you're here tonight."

"I'd like to be here every night."

He stood up, ignoring her last statement. She watched him undress, fascinated by his tall, muscular body, his wide shoulders. He flung his Levi's at the chair, missed. He slid his shorts over his hips, let them fall to his feet and then kicked them in the direction of his rumpled clothes. She was amazed that he was ready for her so quickly. His rigid stalk curved upward, wavered back and forth, as he came to her.

"You don't need this," he said, sliding her soft pink nightgown up, over his head. Her large firm breasts jutted out, begging to be caressed. He leaned over the lantern, curled his hand around the top of the glass and blew into it. In the darkness, he savored the delicate scent of soap and toilet water, the sound of rustling cloth and heavy breathing. He slid into bed, felt the magnetism radiate from her warm bare flesh.

Bolt found her soft, sensuous lips with his own, parted them with his tongue. He cupped his hand around an ample breast, squeezed it tenderly. She welcomed his kiss, his touch. She thrust her hips upward, a hunger clawing deep inside her loins.

Her hand moved from his wide shoulder to the curly hair on his chest, snaked down across his belly. It traced a path down to his things like a snail. Long, graceful fingers touched his swollen shaft, shooting tiny electric shocks through his flesh.

"Oh, Bolt," she sighed, "you're so . . . so big."

She wrapped her slender fingers around the base of his cock, slid them up the length of it until the skin folded over the sensitive mushroom head.

"Ummm, that feels good," Bolt husked. "Cassie, you're the best woman in Abilene."

He bent his head down to her creamy breast, took the nipple into his mouth and suckled it. He massaged the spongy breast gently as he tongued the nipple to hardness. He let his hand roam the valleys and hills of her curves until he found her secret place. When he touched the bare flesh of her thighs, near her sensuous pussy, she gasped with pleasure.

"Does that feel good?" he asked.

"Yes, oh yes, right there. Touch me right there," she moaned when his fingers lingered at the folds of her sex. She slid her cupped fingers up and down the length of his erection, moving them faster as she became more excited. He rubbed her damp portal, parted her lips and pushed his finger into the steaming cauldron. She thrust her body upward, taking his finger in deep.

"Oh, Bolt, I want you. Now. I want you inside me, my love."

Glistening fluid leaked from the eye of his penis tip. She lovingly dabbed at it, smeared the slippery substance around its sensitive head.

"I want you, too, Cassie."

Bolt was more than ready. He was so hot, he couldn't wait any longer to plunge his spear into her sheath. He positioned himself above her widespread thighs, his rigid cock wavering from side to side. He lowered himself, pushed his warhead against her splayed lips, penetrated her moist cunt with deliberate slowness. He felt tight muscles lock around his penis, holding him deep in the cave of pleasure.

She groaned. "Oh stop! Wait! I'm coming! I'm commmmmmming!"

He paused, felt her muscles spasm against his stiff rod. He was grateful for the delay because he was on the verge of exploding with his own orgasm. After a moment, he began stroking her deeply, pulling his cock almost out of her, then inserting it again. Deep into the honey. She rocked up and down, matching his rhythm, thrusting upward when he stroked her. His throbbing rod made contact with all of her sensitive spots, rubbed against her clitoris as he penetrated her. He brought her to the point of ecstasy again. She purred like a kitten, wriggling beneath him. They were one, in harmony with the universe. He hesitated, held himself back. She wrapped her arms around his bare shoulders, squeezed him tightly as she shuddered with another orgasm.

He plunged into her again, slowly at first, then speeded up as he neared the pinnacle of excitement. He exploded deep inside her, his milky fluid splashing against the walls of her cavern. For one brief moment, everything was blotted from his consciousness except pure pleasure.

"It was good, Cassie. You're good."

They held each other closely, basking in the afterglow of lovemaking, contented. Silence engulfed the room as shreds of early-morning light filtered through the curtains. Finally, Bolt rolled off her body and stretched out on the bed. He folded his hands behind his head, his arms bent to wings.

He could not stop the flow of images that intruded upon his mind. He thought about the men he had killed the night before, wondered why, at twenty-three, he was a hunted man — an outlaw, always keeping one jump ahead of bounty hunters and cocky gunmen. He had been on the run for five long years, not from the gunnies at first, but from a gal, a damned horny, possessive bitch. Amy Robinson. He had carried his resentments for her for a long time, blamed her for all his troubles.

Amy had seduced him when he was eighteen, back in 1870. She was twenty-two at the time, he remembered, four years older than he and more experienced about such matters. It had been good and exciting the first couple of times and he guessed he liked sex as well as anyone else. But then she started demanding sex from him whenever she got horny. She hadn't really forced him to make love to her, but she had threatened to tell everyone at church that he had raped her if he didn't perform at her beck and call. Then she had gone and gotten herself in a family way, blamed him for it. It made for a sticky situation since Jared's father was the local preacher and Amy's father was the choirmaster. Everyone thought Amy was so damned pure because she sang in the choir. Bullshit. When his preacher father Elijah found out about it, Bolt found himself headed for a shotgun wedding.

That's when he and his good friend, Tom Penrod, decided to light a shuck from Ellsworth, Kansas, make their own way in the rugged west.

Tom had been wanting to leave him for a long time. His old man was a farmer who drank too much and spent the weekends in town, squandering his money on whores. His mother did a little hand-sewing and baking just to keep food on the table.

Tom Penrod and Jared Bolt found work where they could, did odd jobs to keep their bellies full and a roof over their heads. They worked as ranch hands for a while. It was hard work, but it kept them in good physical shape. They finally accumulated a herd of cattle and became drovers.

Jared's brother, Michael had been tracking Jared all these years, trying to persuade Jared to go back to Ellsworth and marry Amy Robinson. But Michael had been too inept to exert any authority.

There had been other women since Amy. Some good ones, like Cassie Owens, some bad ones, too. Seemed like they always caused him trouble though. Like Belinda Wilkins. Damned if that hadn't been a mess. Belinda had run away from her husband Reed, who was one mean *hombre*. Reed had caught Bolt in bed with Belinda, tried to kill Bolt, and Bolt killed Reed, in self defense. Then when Reed's brother, Marshal Maynard Wilkins, came after Bolt, there had been a shootout that left Maynard and two others dead. Now, the Wilkins brothers' father, Judge Wilkins over in Coffeyville, was sending bounty hunters after him.

It wasn't only Wilkins who was after his ass. That cheating banker Norvell wanted a piece of the action. That pipsqueak Norvell had swindled Tom and him out of their cattle money. Well, they got the money back all right, but they had to take it from Norvell's bank in Fort Scott at gunpoint. Norvell had been madder than hell since he'd been humiliated in front of his employees.

A smile crossed Bolt's lips when he thought of the look on old man Norvell's face. The banker hadn't wasted any time sending gunnies after him. Posters sprang up all over Fort Scott offering $1000 reward for the capture of "bank robbers Jared Bolt and Tom Penrod." So Bolt and his partner were outlaws according to society, with a price on their heads.

Home to Bolt these days was his own whorehouse in Abilene, Kansas, won fair and square in a poker game with a degenerate gambler. Irishman Paddy Killeen, former owner of the Drover's Saloon, left town deeply in debt, after losing to Bolt. Bolt changed the name of the combination hotel, saloon and whorehouse to Bolt's Bawdy House, an act that caused the townspeople some consternation.

"Something bothering you, Bolt?"

The soft voice brought Bolt back to the present.

"Nope. Just thinkin'." He ran a hand over Cassie's smooth bare flesh.

"You're so quiet," she said.

"Did Tom come back home last night?"

"Yes. I heard him come in about midnight. I came to your room shortly after that. Tom wasn't out late."

"Don't take him long to finish his . . . ah . . . business. I swear, that feller's going to squander every cent he has on whores."

"You shouldn't complain, Bolt. After all, you make your living off of whores now, same as Barney over at the Devil's Addition."

"That's not true, Cassie," Bolt protested. "I merely provide a service for the men in need. Can't help it if there's a profit in it. I treat my gals like ladies. They get good pay. Besides, I don't own the girls. They're free to come and go as they wish. They can leave anytime they please."

"I know, Bolt. They've never been treated like ladies before. They like you. They really do."

"Well, I need to talk to Tom as soon as he's awake."

"About what?" She knew Bolt well enough to know when something was upsetting him.

Bolt hesitated before he went on. "You're gonna find out about it anyway, probably, but I'd like to keep it quiet. I had to kill a couple of gunnies last night. Bounty hunters. They were waitin' for me in the field near the stockyards when I come back from the Alamo. Three of 'em. One of 'em got away. A guy named Will Atterbury."

"Oh, Bolt, that's terrible. How do you know his name?"

"I have ways." He cocked his head, grinned at her. "I been up against this guy before. Only he was a Jayhawker then. Thinks he's hot shit, but he's got a yellow streak down his back a mile long."

"I wish they'd leave you alone. You shouldn't have hung that sign out front advertising Bolt's Bawdy House, you know. It's like announcing, 'Here I am. Come and get me.' Besides, the people in town don't like that sign. They think it's undignified, obscene, a blight to the village."

"Fuck the town people. I believe in honesty. I call a spade a spade. Those damn Sunday Christians, the other prominent men in town. They're the ones who're screaming the loudest and they're the very ones who are using the services I provide. They just don't like the pressure they're gettin' from their prissy wives."

"Are you going to hide out?"

"Hell no. I don't back down to no man. I just like to meet 'em on my own terms, that's all. I won't have to worry about bounty hunters for a while, I reckon. It'll take a few days for word to get back about those two out in the field."

"What are you going to do now, Bolt?"

"Same thing I been doing. Enjoy life. Live every minute of it."

"Bolt, you're something." Her laughter tinkled through the room. "You do enjoy life, don't you?"

"Sure, why not? Hey, I'm the luckiest man around. I got my own whorehouse."

"Damn you, Bolt. I can't tell when you're serious or when you're teasing me. Now, seriously, what are you going to do?"

"The first thing I'm going to do is spruce this place up a bit." He kept his tone light hearted.

"Bolt, you're impossible," she laughed.

"Hey, I'm serious, Cassie. You know what I'm going to do tomorrow?"

"It's already tomorrow," she said, glancing at the window where daylight streamed through the curtains.

"First, I'm going to order some new curtains and bed linens from the Monkey Ward Catalog. And second, I'm going to make love to you all day long."

"Oh, Bolt," she laughed. "I love you."

"Of course you do. Now, do you want to help me?"

"With which project, Bolt? Picking curtains out or making love?" she teased, wiggling her body closer to Bolt.

"Both."

"You'd better get some sleep. You're randy."

When she hopped out of bed, he studied her naked body, wanted her again. But, his tiredness caught up with him. He fell asleep before she was dressed. She gathered up her nightgown, put it in a small satchel, then left his room, closing the door quietly behind her.

\* \* \* \* \* \* \* \* \* \*

Some two hundred miles away, a stranger rode down the dusty main street of Coffeyville, Kansas. He studied the signs on the falsefronts in town, found the one he was looking for. Judge Advocate, Judge Andrew Jackson Wilkins. The Texan stopped in front of the small log building, dismounted and tied his horse to the hitchrail. He brushed dust and grime from his clothes, stretched his tall frame to six feet.

Inside, he removed his hat, ran a hand through his greased-down hair. A short, stocky woman greeted him.

"May I help you, sir?"

He told the clerk only his name and that he wanted to see the judge. She rose from the desk, her large full breasts straining against the material of her dress. She walked to a door near the rear of the room, opened it, entered and closed the door behind her.

The stranger stood, legs apart, hat craddled under one arm. His cold, dark brown eyes scanned the room quickly, absorbing every detail. It was his nature to do this. He had a reputation in Texas. As an expert bounty hunter. The best in the west.

A small sign amid the clutter of papers on the desk told him that the clerk's name was Mollie Appleton. He didn't know much about this man they called Bolt, but before he was through, he would know more about the man than he knew about himself. He'd keep his reputation. He'd never failed to get a man he went after and he didn't aim to fail now. Bolt would be a real challenge. Bolt had a reputation of his own.

A moment later, Miss Appleton reappeared.

"Judge Wilkins will see you now, Mr. Fisher."

## CHAPTER THREE

He would have slept past noon if someone hadn't knocked on his door. Bolt roused from a deep sleep, shook his head to clear the cobwebs.

"It's me. Tom. You in there, Bolt?"

"Yeah, just a minute."

Bolt stepped into his Levi's, opened the door. Tom Penrod walked in, looking fresh and well-rested. He was a little shorter than Bolt, a little ganglier. His mop of tousled brown hair always looked the same, like he'd just crawled out of bed. Sometimes people thought Bolt and Tom were brothers. But Tom's hair was dark brown, Bolt's coal black, sleek. Tom had hazel eyes that tended to take on the color of his surroundings, sometimes appearing brown, sometimes blue. There was no doubting the color of Bolt's eyes. They were pure blue, as blue as the sky.

"Cassie said you wanted to see me," said Tom.

"Yeah. We got problems, Tom. Did she tell you about it?"

"No. Just said you wanted to see me."

"Good. I knew I could trust her. I told her I wanted it kept quiet." Bolt walked over to the dresser, poured water from a pitcher into the porcelain bowl. He cupped his hands together and splashed water on his face, ran his wet hands through his hair. He reached for the bar of soap and scrubbed his hands, dipped them into the bowl to rinse them.

"What kind of problems?" Penrod asked.

"Sit down, will ya?"

Tom pulled a wooden chair over close to the bed, plopped down in it and stretched his long legs out so his feet rested on the end of the bed. He got a slight whiff of Cassie's perfume that lingered in the air. Bolt pulled a clean shirt from the curtained closet, put it on.

"I got jumped by three gunnies last night. The bastards. I bagged two of 'em, but the third one got away, ran like a scared piss ant. Will Atterbury. Remember him? Too dark to get a good shot at him."

"Shit," said Tom. "They're closing in on us."

"Think old Judge Wilkins sent 'em our way. At least that's what Bull Bob told me last night. Wilkins wants revenge for the deaths of his bastard sons and he's aimin' to see my neck in a noose. You'd never get a fair trial from that sonofabitch. He's as crooked as his two sons were."

When Bolt finished dressing, they walked to the dining room, which was almost full that time of day. Bolt eyed every customer as they made their way to a corner table. Force of habit. He was always on the lookout for suspicious looking strangers.

A pleasant woman came toward them, a muslin apron tied around her plump body.

"Good morning, Tessie," Bolt said.

"Good afternoon, Mr. Bolt, Mr. Penrod. Beautiful day. What would you like? I'm cooking beef stew and I got a good meat loaf in the oven."

"Can you fix me a big, thick steak, Tessie? Nice and juicy."

"Sure can. No trouble at all."

"Good. I'd like a couple of fried eggs with it, some biscuits and gravy. I'd like a glass of milk, too."

"Sounds good to me," said Tom. "I'll have the same thing, Tessie, although it's hard to pass up your meat loaf."

"Ah, bless your heart. You boys want coffee while you're waiting?"

"Yes, please," said Bolt. Tom nodded. Tessie disappeared into the kitchen and returned a minute later, juggling two clean cups and saucers in one hand, a pot of steaming coffee in the other. She poured the coffee, left the pot on the table.

Bolt filled Tom in on the events of the night before, talking in a low voice so no one would hear him.

"Looks bad," Tom said, shaking his head. "Think Atterbury's still on our tail?"

"I don't think so. He ain't got balls enough to face us alone. We got a little time to breathe. It'll take a while for the word to spread. But, I been thinkin'. It's about time we move on. I still want to go over to Dodge City, look over the place. See if we can find a nice ranch and settle down for awhile. I might even buy me another whorehouse. Never kin tell."

"I'm for that. I'll sample the girls first to be sure you're gettin' a square deal." Penrod leaned back in his chair, balanced on two legs and roared with laughter.

"You're gonna wear your pecker down to a nub," kidded Bolt. He could feel the eyes staring at them as other diners bobbed their heads toward the laughter.

Tessie's timing was perfect. She waddled out of the kitchen, a plate heaped with food in each hand. She set the plates down on the checkered tablecloth. She made another trip to the kitchen and returned with a tray which held two glasses of milk, a napkin-covered basket of freshly baked biscuits and a bowl of brown gravy.

"You're a saint, Tessie," said Bolt.

"Yes, sir. A saint of hungry scoundrels, that's what I am."

Tom and Bolt kept their conversation to a minimum while they ate. Tom finished eating first, pushed his chair back and rolled a cigarette.

"That was good," he said.

Bolt sopped up the last bit of gravy with a biscuit, wiped a napkin across his mouth. "Remind me to give Tessie a raise."

"What's that about a raise?" Cassie had walked up to their table just in time to hear Bolt's last remark.

"Pull up a chair, Cassie," Bolt said. He stood up half way and pulled out a chair for her. She looked even more beautiful than she had earlier that morning, if that was possible. Her long blue dress reflected the color of her eyes. Her dark shiny hair was pulled away from her face, tied with a blue ribbon in back and fell gracefully to her shoulders. Tom smelled the same scent of Cassie's perfume that he had sniffed earlier in Bolt's room. She was one woman he'd like to take to his bed. But he wouldn't. She was Bolt's girl. Sort of.

"Bolt was just saying he was going to give Tessie a raise," Tom said. He smiled at Cassie, stared into her blue eyes. She held Tom's gaze for a long moment. He thought he detected an invitation in her look. Her lips curled into a sensuous smile.

Tom pushed away from the table, stood up.

"I think I'll do a little scouting around. See if any strangers are in town."

Cassie and Bolt spent the next half hour picking out the items they wanted from the Montgomery Ward catalog Cassie had brought. Besides the white muslin sheets for every bed in the place and colorful print curtains, they picked out red and white checked oil cloth to make new tablecloths for the dining room tables.

"I'd like to talk to the girls," Bolt said when they were finished. "Think you can round them up?"

"Will do. They should all be up and about by now."

Bolt strolled over to the bar, greeted the men who sat there guzzling beer and whiskey. A couple of them looked like hardcases. Probably on the run, same as he and Tom. Bolt didn't care. As long as they didn't cause any problems in his place.

Bolt sat at the end of the bar, ordered a whiskey from Alec Lean.

"It's quiet today, Bolt," said the bartender when he served the whiskey.

"I like it that way." Bolt studied the customers, was curious about where they came from. He wondered why some folks turned bad while others were able to remain quiet and honest amid the lawlessness of the vast west. He thought about the six girls who worked at his establishment, earning their living in the world's oldest profession. What made these girls become prostitutes? They weren't really bad girls. At least most of them. Sometimes they would subject themselves to the cruelties of mean men. Drunk, ugly men. Maybe there was no mystery to it at all. Maybe the girls just enjoyed sex. Hell, he didn't know.

One thing he did know — they had a reputation to live with. Same as he did. It wasn't fair, he thought, to lump all whores in one bag and call them "dirty." No more fair than to call every man who had killed another, an outlaw.

One young man at the bar interested Bolt more than the others. Bolt guessed him to be about eighteen or nineteen. Clean but shabby clothes covered his tall, thin body. His blonde hair was just as shabby, hung to his shoulders. His pale blue eyes were what bothered Bolt, though. They had a look of hunger about them, or maybe of fear. He didn't appear to be a hardcase and as far as Bolt could tell, he wasn't carrying a piece. He didn't look like a ranch hand or a cowboy either. His slender hands were too smooth.

The boy at the bar had a beer in front of him, but he wasn't drinking much of it. He seemed restless, didn't talk to anyone. It wasn't long before the stranger stood up, walked away from the bar. Bolt looked in the mirror behind the bar, watched the reflection of the young man as he moved across the room, pulled out the piano stool and sat down.

He plunked out a few notes on the keyboard, then picked out a tune that was familiar to Bolt. The kid stopped playing for a moment, looked down at the keyboard, then began playing with complete control. Chopin. Bolt was amazed that the young man who looked like a drifter could play so well.

Interested, Bolt walked over, pulled a chair close to the piano and sat on it backwards, his legs straddling the seat, his chin resting on folded hands.

The music flowed effortlessly as slender fingers flew through intricate passages. When the boy stopped playing, he looked over at Bolt, a quizzical smile on his lips.

"You like it?" he asked softly.

"You play mighty good," Bolt said.

"Thanks."

"My name's Bolt. You from around here?"

"I'm Danny Eperwinkle. Nope, just passing through."

"Where'd you learn to play like that? You're really good, Dan."

"My mama taught me. I been playing the piano since I was five."

"Where you headed?"

That same hungry, faraway look came into Dan's eyes.

"Well, Mr. Bolt, I'm going to California. San Francisco. Soon's I can afford it."

"You lookin' for work?"

"Well, I don't know. I guess so. My mama always wanted to go to San Francisco. She died a month ago. She was awful sick before she died and she made me promise her that I'd take the money she had saved and go to San Francisco. Only problem is, the stage coach I was riding in was robbed. Them robbers took all my mama's money. She worked all her life to save that money. My papa, he died during the war. I hardly even knew him. I was six years old when he died and my mama gave piano lessons to earn that money. Now it's all gone. But I'll get to San Francisco. I promised my mama."

All the grief that Dan had held inside himself flooded out as he talked to Bolt. Tears clouded his pale blue eyes. Bolt liked the kid. He had spunk.

"How would you like to stay on here, Dan? For a while? I'd like to hire you to play the piano for the evening crowd. Abilene's a rough town, but no rougher than some others, I reckon. I'll give you a decent salary, a place to stay and all the food you can eat. That piano's been idle for a long time. We could sure use you. What do you say?"

"Gee, Mr. Bolt, I'd like that."

"Good." Bolt reached in his pocket, pulled out two twenty dollar bills. "Just call me Bolt. Here, go get some new duds and a haircut. You hungry?"

"I sure am, Bolt."

"Come on with me. I'll introduce you to Tessie. She'll fix you up."

Bolt led Dan into the kitchen, made the introductions.

"Tessie, we're going to have music in this place. Dan's really good."

"Well, glory be. It's about time," smiled Tessie. "Now don't you worry. I'll cook you up something real good, Dan."

A half an hour later, Tessie delivered the food to the table where Dan and Bolt were talking. Bolt excused himself when Cassie entered the room. Bolt made a quick introduction before he and Cassie walked over to the corner table in the back of the room.

"The girls are on their way, Bolt. Be down in a minute."

A few minutes later, Bolt saw five of the glitter gals come into the room.

"Annie will be here in a little while," said Linda. "She was swimming in the Smokey Hill River and had to change into dry clothes."

"Again?" grinned Bolt. He had heard the rumors about Annie skinny dipping with her customers.

"Let's go to the back room," suggested Bolt. He stood up and glanced at Dan. He noticed that Dan was staring goggle-eyed at the girls. Bolt was willing to bet that Dan had never had a piece of ass in his life. He'd have some growing up to do.

Bolt sat at the big wooden desk in the room he called the office. The girls pulled straight chairs around in a semi-circle in front of Bolt. Cassie sat in the first chair on Bolt's right. Wanda brought her chair up on Bolt's left, as close as she could.

Bolt glanced around at the girls, waited until Annie arrived before he started his talk.

Wanda looked much better, Bolt thought, without all that heavy makeup that she wore at night. In fact, she was a very pretty girl. A little on the plump side, but she had nice facial features. When she wore the heavy rouge, she looked much older than her eighteen years.

Bolt thought back to the first night he and Tom had come into this saloon, the night he had won it in a poker game with Paddy Killeen. Wanda had approached him that night, felt scorned when he turned her down. He had told her that he had a rule that he wouldn't ever pay for a woman's favors. He had another rule now. He never slept with any of the girls who worked for him. It could cause problems that he didn't care to deal with. Besides, Cassie was enough woman for him right now. She wasn't one of the glitter gals, but acted as their housemother. She saw to their needs, kept them out of trouble.

Wanda never stopped trying to get Bolt in bed, though, and sometimes her jealous streak flared up at Cassie in the form of crude remarks.

Linda was the youngest of the six girls who worked at the Bawdy House. She was sixteen and tried to hide her youth by wearing globs of makeup. But there was no way she could hide her mammoth breasts and callipygean buttocks. She was in love with Tom, but Tom liked variety and often visited the Addition.

When Annie swished in, the girls were all giggly. She took a seat in the middle of the others.

"First of all," Bolt began, "I'd like to tell you that I'm going to raise your salary to $300 a month." The girls cheered in unison. Bolt raised a hand for silence. "That's more than the others around here make, but we can afford it. The main thing is that I want you all to be happy. I want you treated with respect. I don't own you, you know. I want you to understand that. You are always free to leave when you want to. If you ever have any trouble with the men, let me know. I'm here to protect you. Cassie's here to help you with your problems."

"Huh," muttered Wanda.

Bolt looked at her, saw that she was glaring across at Cassie.

"You got something to say, Wanda?" asked Bolt.

"Cassie might be able to help you with your problems, but not mine."

The other girls giggled at Wanda's suggestive remark.

"If you've got a problem, you come to me with it." Bolt said curtly. "We've ordered new sheets and curtains for your rooms. And, I just hired a piano player, Dan Eperwinkle. I'm going to clear a space for dancing. We're going to make this the best whorehouse in the west. Do any of you have any questions?"

There was no response.

"Now, get some rest. Look pretty tonight. We're going to dazzle the customers."

He stood up, dismissing the girls. They filed out of the room, chattering like a flock of magpies.

Wanda held back, waited until the others were gone.

"I've got a problem," Wanda said. She snuggled in close to Bolt, pushed her large breasts against him. "You said you'd take care of it."

He felt desire flood his loins as she wriggled against him. He wanted very much to take Wanda to bed. Especially without the gaudy makeup she usually wore.

But he wouldn't.

"I'm sorry, Wanda, but I can't. Against the rules, you know," he said lightly.

"You mean you won't," she pouted. "To hell with your rules. Cassie's got you right where she wants you — wrapped around her little finger."

"That's not true, Wanda." He put his arm around her, patted her shoulder.

"Yes it is true! She's no better'n me."

"You're both very fine women, Wanda. Don't ever forget that."

They walked out of the room locked arm in arm.

The bat wing doors swung open. A tall man stood there in the doorway, his arms folded in front of him. Sunlight streaming in from outside made the man look like a shadowy ghost. Bolt squinted his eyes. A shock of recognition jolted his senses. His face blanched ashen.

It was a ghost.

Out of his past.

## CHAPTER FOUR

Bolt regained his composure. He stood there for a moment, not knowing what to say to the old man standing in the doorway. Finally, he walked over to the gray-haired man, his arms extended. He was shocked to see how much his father had aged in the last five years. Wrinkles lined the man's face.

"Father. It's been a long time. Come on in."

Reverend Elijah Bolt stood as firm as an Indian Chief, his folded arms snugged in tightly to his chest. It was obvious that he had no intention of sharing his son's embrace.

Bolt tensed involuntarily from the rejection, then quickly shook off the hurt that stabbed at his heart.

"Come in, Father, and sit down."

Elijah Bolt glared at his son.

"I will not enter this house of sin. I am shocked and appalled that you have gotten yourself involved in this place that condones drinking, gambling and prostitution. I will not set foot inside a place that is the work of the devil."

"Father, please...."

"Be still, Jared. I need to talk to you. I would ask you to join me for supper tonight so that we might talk. I have just ridden in a little while ago. I am staying at Jensen's Boarding House in town and must leave for home early in the morning. Will you have supper with me tonight at Mrs. Jensen's?"

"Yes, Father, I'll be there."

"Fine, Jared. Dinner is served promptly at six." He turned abruptly and walked away.

A feeling of sadness came over Bolt as he watched his father walk away. He wished he could explain all the feelings inside him, the joy he felt for life, but his father would not understand. He wasn't sure he understood these feelings himself.

Bolt had long ago forgiven his father for beating him within an inch of his life on that day five years ago when the preacher had found Jared and Amy Robinson together in the hay loft. Bolt had tried to explain that day that Amy had seduced him, but that didn't matter to Elijah. The preacher believed that everything was black or white, right or wrong. As far as he was concerned there was only one side to every situation — his side. Bolt could never understand how his father could preach about a forgiving God and yet be so unforgiving himself.

\* \* \* \* \* \* \* \* \* \*

When Bolt and his father finished the meal that they shared with other diners at the boarding house, they went up to Elijah's room to talk privately.

"Sit down, my son."

The room was like so many others Bolt had seen, except it was better cared for. Two small rugs hid portions of the highly polished hardwood floors; one by the bed, the other in front of the dresser. A colorful quilt covered the feather bed. Landscape prints hung on the walls.

Jared sat down, his fingers tracing the pattern carved in the arms of the rocking chair. He was uncomfortable with his father. He felt like a little boy who'd been caught with his hand in the cookie jar. Elijah paced the floor, stopped in front of Jared, glared at him.

"Son, you must give up your evil ways and come home with me."

"Father, I . . . ."

"None of your excuses. You have an obligation to marry Amy Robinson and make her son legitimate. Give the boy a name. I came here to insist that you come home and face your responsibilities. Your brother Michael is very upset by the way you treated him when he found you. He is on the verge of a nervous breakdown. He is not strong like you, Jared."

"He shouldn't have tracked me down, Father. I have my own life to live."

"That is not true. You have obligations. You must come home. You must repent. Amy has lived in shame all these years. You owe it to her to marry her. And I have lived with the shame of your sins, too. You must clear our name with my parishioners."

"I think that's all you're concerned about, Father, your damned name. You're only thinking of yourself."

Bolt tried to control his temper. He didn't want to hurt his father any more than he had already been hurt.

"No, Jared, I'm thinking of Amy and that poor boy she is raising by herself. People are still talking about how you deserted her. You have sinned."

"Father, I will never marry Amy. She made her own bed."

"God will punish you."

It was obvious that Bolt could not reach his father. The old man was stubborn, almost as stubborn as he was.

Elijah continued to pace back and forth, ranting on about how evil Jared was, how he must save his soul before it was too late. The preacher was full of fire and brimstone. Suddenly, he stopped in front of his son, pulled a tattered piece of paper from his pocket and threw it in Bolt's lap.

"It's bad enough the way my people talk about you and Amy. Now they're talking about this too!"

Bolt looked at the paper. It was a clipping torn from the *Ellsworth Reporter*, dated September 20, 1875. Bolt read the words framed by a dark border. "Wanted, dead or alive, Jared Bolt and Tom Penrod, for murder and bank robbery. Reward: $2000."

"It's not what it looks like, Father," Jared protested. "I can explain."

The preacher held up a hand for silence, cutting Bolt off once again.

"No need to explain. The facts are right there for everyone to see. When I saw this notice in last week's paper, I knew I had to come myself to bring you back. I am so ashamed of you. I hope God can forgive you your sins."

"Father, I. . . ."

Elijah turned his back on his son, again paced to the door and back. He stood above Bolt, his blue eyes full of sadness. He cleared his throat, wrung his veined hands.

"I am getting old, son. I have not been well lately. I don't think I will live very much longer and I want to have peace of mind before I go. I beg you to repent, come home now and set things right with the Lord."

Bolt watched his father and stifled a smile. His father was a consumate actor. The fire and brimstone tactics hadn't worked, so now he was appealing to Jared's sympathies. Well, that wouldn't work either. He could rave and rant, cry, beg, anything he wanted and Jared would never change his mind.

Bolt softened toward his father, felt sorry for him, in a way. The old man worried his life away.

"I will go to Ellsworth soon, Father. I promise. To see you and Michael. But I will not marry Amy."

Elijah sat down on the edge of the bed, put his head in his hands. He rubbed his forehead as if to smooth the wrinkles away. He knew he had pushed his son as far as he could right now. Perhaps if Jared came to Ellsworth he would realize the need to marry Amy. He looked up at his son, his pale blue eyes reflecting the sadness in his heart.

"I will pray for you, my son."

Jared wanted to hold his father in his arms, assure him that everything was all right. He stood up, walked over to the bed and rested a hand on his father's shoulder.

"Father, I must go now. Please get some rest before you go back home tomorrow."

Elijah stood up, reached out and pulled Jared into his embrace, then released him quickly.

"Go with God, my son."

"You, too, Father."

Jared was gone before his father could say any more. He stepped out into the chilly night air, mounted his bay.

A tiredness settled in his bones as he rode toward home in the moonlit night. The meeting with his father had drained everything out of him. An uneasiness gripped him as he passed by the tall trees that loomed up by the side of the road near the open field. He kicked his horse in the flanks, urged it to a gallop.

\*\*\*\*\*\*\*\*\*\*

Business was booming at Bolt's Bawdy House. It had been more than a week since young Dan Eperwinkle began playing the piano for the evening crowds.

Bolt's father had left Abilene the morning after the two of them had talked. He hadn't stopped to see his son before he left as Bolt had hoped.

"We've got a live one at the bar, Bolt," Tom Penrod said in a hushed voice.

Bolt was leaning against a post, watching the action at the poker tables, thinking about his father. On busy nights, like tonight, he and Tom kept close tabs on the place, trying to spot trouble before it happened.

"He's pretty drunk," Tom continued. "Think he's spoiling for a fight. Do you want me to toss him out on his ass?"

"Who is it?" Bolt glanced in the direction of the bar.

"Bob Steckley."

"His ole man own Steckley Ranch?"

"Yep."

"Just tell Alec to cut him off. No more booze. Let him go someplace else to find a sparring partner."

Tom sauntered back to the bar, caught Alec's eye.

"No more whiskey for the loud mouth."

"Yes, sir," said Alec, his eyes drifting toward the drunk.

Steckley banged his glass on the polished bartop.

"Another whiskey," he demanded.

"Sorry, sir," Alec said politely, "the boss says you've had enough."

The tall muscular man stood up, infuriated.

"You refusin' me a drink?" he slurred.

"That's right."

Steckley's hand fumbled for his pistol. He looked up, spotted Bolt standing ten feet behind him, his hand hovering above his holster. He shoved his pistol back in the holster, grabbed his hat off the bar and jammed it on his head. He staggered toward the door, tripped on a chair and stumbled against the piano.

"Well, lookey here. A sissy piano player," he said in a loud voice. Look at them del-eee-cate hands. I bet they never stroked a woman's behind."

Dan cringed on the piano stool.

"In fact, I bet this sissy don't know what a good piece of ass is." He laughed loudly, reeled drunkenly on his heels.

Dan came up off the piano stool, his face blood red with rage. He doubled his fist and landed an upper cut to the drunk's chin. Steckley toppled over like a bail of hay, landed on his back. He tried to get up.

Bolt stepped in, grabbed him by the collar, pulled him straight up in the air. He pushed him against the piano, jerked him by the hair and the seat of the britches toward the door. With one hard kick, he booted the drunk out the door.

"Don't ever show your face in here again!"

"No one refuses me a drink. I'll get you for this, Bolt, you bastard!"

Bolt turned around, brushed his hands together as if to get rid of dust and dirt. The crowd cheered and then went back to drinking and gambling.

"You okay?" Bolt asked Dan.

"My hand hurts a little."

"His jaw's as hard as his thick head. Next time try for the belly. It's softer," Bolt kidded. He could see that Dan was shook up.

"I . . . I'm sorry. I didn't mean to cause any trouble."

"Not your fault."

Wanda, who had been sitting nearby, ran over to Dan.

"Dan, are you hurt?"

"No, not really."

"Let me look at your hand," Bolt said. He ran his thumb and forefinger along the length of the bruised fingers. Dan winced when Bolt touched the two middle fingers.

"You'd better take the rest of the night off, Dan. Take care of that hand."

"I've got some salts up in my room," said Wanda. "Come on, Dan, I'll take care of you."

She looped her arm in Dan's and led him away. She stuck her nose in the air, threw Bolt a hauty look.

Bolt knew that tonight Dan would have more than his hand taken care of.

\* \* \* \* \* \* \* \* \* \*

The banker eyed the neatly dressed man who had been ushered into his office.

"My name is Chad Fisher. I need some information."

"Horatio P. Norvell. Please sit down."

The heavy set man was president of the Fort Scott Bank & Trust Company. The vest he wore under his dark pin-striped suit bulged at the buttons. He was bald except for small patches of speckled hair on either side of his head. His mutton-chop beard was the same color as his sparse hair.

Chad Fisher scrutinized the older man, took note of the heavy rings adorning the banker's short stubby fingers, the gold watch chain hanging from the vest pocket. The odor of cigars and brandy were not hidden by the strong toilet water he wore.

"What kind of information you want, Mr. Fisher?"

"Everything you can tell me about a man named Bolt."

Fisher noticed the banker stiffen at the mention of Bolt's name. Norvell put his hands out flat on the desk in front of him, nervous fingers clanking the rings against the smooth surface.

"What's your connection with Mr. Bolt?"

"I understand Bolt robbed your bank, Mr. Norvell. I'm a hunter. A very good one, I might add. Need I say more?"

"Yes, I understand. Yes, he did rob my bank, at gunpoint. He and his friend, Penrod."

"I also heard that you bought cattle from him and short changed him." Fisher's cold dark eyes glared into Norvell's.

"You heard wrong, Mr. Fisher. I paid them cash before I took delivery. They just got greedy, that's all."

Chad's smile went undetected. He wouldn't trust Norvell as far as he could throw him, but that was beyond the point. All he wanted was information.

"What do you know about him?"

"He's a tough man, a killer. A hard man to get. Likely you'll have trouble with him." Norvell didn't like Fisher any better than Fisher liked him.

"You know where I can find him?"

"He's in Abilene now. Or at least he was a week ago. He owns a whorehouse there. Won it in a poker game, I hear. Was probably cheating."

"From what I hear, Bolt doesn't need to cheat." The remark was meant to be sarcastic.

The chair creaked as Norvell swiveled it.

"There's a man you should meet. Will Atterbury. He just came back from Abilene yesterday. He's a bounty hunter, like yourself. He went after Bolt. Only he came back empty handed and minus two of his friends."

"I can assure you, Mr. Norvell. I will get Bolt. I *always* get the man I go after."

"I hope so. I want to see that thief dead."

The Texan pulled himself up in the chair, leaned forward.

"That brings me to another point. Are you prepared to offer reward money to see Bolt dead?"

"There's already a bounty reward of two thousand dollars."

"I know. That money was offered by concerned citizens, not you. Judge Wilkins wants Bolt alive. To stand trial in his court. He's willing to pay me an extra thousand."

"Ha. Fat chance Bolt'd get with Wilkins as the judge. I already put up some of the bounty money anyway," protested Norvell.

"You mean your bank did. Didn't come out of your pocket. You want Bolt dead or not?"

"Dead. He's caused me too much humiliation."

"That's what the judge said. Seems like nobody cares about justice."

"You drive a hard bargain, Mr. Fisher. You'll get another two thousand when you deliver Bolt's body."

"It's a deal. Now, where do I find Atterbury?"

"At Fort Scott Hotel. Probably at the bar."

Fisher stood up, tipped his hat.

"Thank you for your time, Mr. Norvell. You'd better be prepared to pay."

Robert Kelley, the short, thin bank teller watched the Texan leave the bank. He fidgeted with his ribbon tie. The twitch in his eye was involuntary.

"Who was that?" asked the nervous teller.

"That was Chad Fisher. A bounty hunter with a reputation."

"He shore don't look like no bounty hunter."

Norvell's lips curled to a wicked smile.

"And that, Mr. Kelly, may just be Bolt's downfall. Bolt has a tendency to trust strangers. He'll be suspicious of every tough gunnie he sees. But when he meets up with Mr. Fisher, he won't suspect a thing."

## CHAPTER FIVE

The brakes screeched, metal ground against metal, as the Kansas Pacific Railroad train approached the small Abilene station. The building that served as a depot was located near the stockyards so that the cattle transported by rail could be easily handled.

Bolt sat on the wooden boardwalk in the shade of the shabby structure. The train was on time, which was unusual. His buckboard sat by the side of the building, next to a fancy horse and buggy. He waited until the train came to a full stop before he got up and stretched his legs.

A short, stocky man emerged from the station, toddled toward the train. It was the station master, Sam Erwin. Following close on his heels was a big blond Swede, Sven Jensen, proprietor of Jensen's Mercantile Store.

"Howdy, Sam," Bolt greeted.

"Hello, Bolt," said the station master. "What brings you out on this fine day?"

"I'm expecting some packages." He turned to the friendly merchant. "Good afternoon, Sven."

"Afternoon, Bolt. Glad the train's here. My brother Olaf and his wife are coming for a visit. Haven't seen them for three years."

The door to the passenger car clanked open. Standing there, framed by the metal door, was the most beautiful creature Bolt had ever seen. A vision in pink. She paused in the doorway a moment, her blue eyes darting around. A large feathery pink hat was perched on top of long blonde hair that cascaded softly around her shoulders.

Behind her in the doorway was a well-dressed gentleman who obviously was Mr. Jensen's brother. The two brothers looked enough alike to be twins.

Mr. Jensen rushed over to the train, offered the pink lady his arm, helped her down the steps. He left her standing there, a small suitcase clutched in one hand, a pink parasol draped over the other. Sven grabbed his brother as Olaf stepped down from the train, embraced him in a bear hug.

"Well, you old coot," Sven said, "you finally made it. Where's Ida?"

"She couldn't come. At the last minute one of the kids took sick."

Bolt was confused. If the lovely lady in pink wasn't Sven's sister-in-law, then who the hell was she?

Sam boarded the train and got back off a minute later, carrying two large satchels. He set them down on the boardwalk, then walked to one of the freight cars.

"I'll get your packages, Bolt," said Sam.

"Thanks."

Bolt looked back over at the pretty lady. She smiled hesitantly at Bolt. Her sensuous lips parted as if she was about to speak. She changed her mind, turned her head.

"Pardon me, ma'am, but are you looking for someone?"

"Well, yes I am. I'm Elizabeth Kendrick. Did you come to pick me up?"

"Not really," Bolt smiled.

Her face flushed with embarrassment.

"Oh, I'm terribly sorry, sir. I thought you were sent from the American Hotel to fetch me. Someone was to meet the train."

"My name is Jared Bolt, ma'am. I'd be glad to give you a ride."

"No thank you," she said curtly, trying to regain her composure.

Bolt walked over and retrieved his packages from Sam as he unloaded them from the train. Bolt carried the heavy bundles to his buckboard, stacked them in the back. He glanced back over at the woman standing alone, shook his head and sauntered back to her.

"Miss Kendrick, I would be happy to take you to the American Hotel. I have my buckboard here."

"Well, I don't know. Someone was to pick me up."

There was something about Bolt's smile that unsettled her, made her blush again. It was sensual, almost sinister. And the way he stared directly at her with his blue eyes.

"If no one shows, Miss, it's a mighty far piece to walk, especially tot'n them bags. Suit yourself." He turned away.

She realized she didn't have any choice in the matter.

"Well, if it wouldn't put you to too much trouble."

"No trouble at all." Bolt picked up the two suitcases, carried them easily, as if they contained feathers. He placed them in the buckboard, next to his packages. He took her arm to help her up, then noticed the dust and grime that covered the seat.

"Just a minute. I'll get something to cover that seat. Your dress is too pretty to ruin on this dirty seat." He grabbed one of his bundles, tore off the wrappings and extracted one brand new, white sheet. She watched him, was curious why he had a box of new sheets. She said nothing.

The buckboard bounced along the rough road as they rode in silence. Elizabeth Kendrick sat tall and prim on the seat, her pink parasol tilted to keep the sun off her face.

"You here to visit, Miss Kendrick?" Bolt said finally.

"No. I'll be staying, sir. I'm the new school marm."

"Good. I hope you like it here."

"It's pretty country, what I've seen of it. Flatter than I'm used to."

The reins stretched tight as Bolt pulled back on them in front of the American Hotel. He helped her down and then lifted her bags carefully out of the buckboard.

"I wish there was some way I could thank you, Mr. Bolt," she said politely.

"How about having dinner with me tonight?"

"Oh, I couldn't possibly. Thank you anyway." Her voice was polite but there was a chilly edge to it. She had heard rumors about the wild men of the west. Her father had warned her to keep her distance.

"How about tomorrow?"

"No, thank you."

"Do you ride, Miss Kendrick?"

"Yes."

"Good. I'll show you the country tomorrow. Do you have a riding outfit?"

"Yes, but. . . ."

"I'll pick you up at one tomorrow afternoon."

She started to protest, but Bolt tipped his hat and strutted back to the buckboard.

"Oh, Miss Kendrick," he called as he climbed onto the seat.

"Yes?"

"I'll bring a picnic supper and a horse for you."

She stood there speechless. She couldn't believe that she had agreed to go riding with a stranger. She hadn't really agreed, but she hadn't said no either. Her father would have a fit if he knew.

She bent down, tried to pick up a suitcase. It was no use. She'd have to get the desk clerk to help her.

* * * * * * * * * *

After breakfast the next morning, Bolt asked Tessie to fix a special box lunch for two. Tessie raised her eyebrows at the request, but didn't ask questions.

"I'll pick it up after noon. Think you can have it ready by then?"

"Yes, Mr. Bolt. I'll fix something nice. It'll be ready."

Bolt leaned over and pecked her on the cheek.

"Thanks, Tessie. You're a sweetheart."

Next Bolt stopped at the empty bar where Alec was preparing for the crowds that would come in a little later.

"What'll you have, Bolt? A whiskey?"

"Nothing now. But I want you to get out our best bottle of champagne. Keep it cool. I'll be back later to get it. I'll need some wet towels, too."

Bolt didn't see much of Cassie that morning. She was busy and he avoided her as much as he could. She was possessive of him and it was best if she didn't know where he was going.

Bolt was sitting at a table talking to Tom when Cassie walked up.

"How do you like the new tablecloths, boys?"

Tom ran his hand over the slick red and white oil cloth, a puzzled look on his face.

"So that's what it is," he said sheepishly. "I knew something was different, but I thought somebody just washed the table."

"You're not too bright," Bolt grinned. "I hear too much screwing causes brain damage."

"You should know," Tom rallied.

"Looks nice, Cassie. You and the girls did a good job."

Tessie's timing couldn't have been worse. She waddled up to the table carrying a box of food.

"There's plenty for two," she said.

"Thanks, Tessie." Bolt avoided Cassie's searching eyes. Bolt silently cursed the smell of fried chicken that drifted in the air.

At 12:30 that afternoon, Bolt mounted his bay and headed for the American Hotel. He would stop at the stables and rent a gentle mare for Miss Kendrick. Full saddlebags hung on the bay's flanks. A bottle of champagne, carefully wrapped in damp towels to keep it cool, was stuffed in one saddlebag, Tessie's special food in the other.

\* \* \* \* \* \* \* \* \* \*

Shortly after Bolt left, three men rode into town.

If Bolt had seen them, he would have been more careful.

He would have recognized two of them.

The three footpads stopped their horses across the street from Bolt's Bawdy House, dismounted. They stayed in the shadows.

"So that's the whorehouse he won in a poker game," said Chad Fisher. "Think he's there now, Steckley?"

"Don't know. Too early for him to be out playing poker."

"Go in and see if he's there," ordered Fisher. "Get him to come outside."

"He won't fall for that," said a rattled but vengeful Will Atterbury. "He's no fool."

"So I've heard," said Chad.

"I'm sure glad you two stopped by my ranch to ask directions to Bolt's Bawdy House," said Steckley. "I want to get that bastard as much as you two do.

Nobody refuses a Steckley a drink and gets away with it."

"We all have our reasons," said Fisher. "Now get going."

Bob Steckley entered the saloon, returned a few minutes later, shaking his head.

"He's not there," said Steckley, "and nobody's talkin'. I asked his girlfriend, Cassie Owens, and she said she didn't know where he was. Then the bartender spotted me. It got kinda sticky in there, so I didn't stay around."

"Cassie Owens, you say?"

"Yeah. Bolt's kinda sweet on her."

Chad Fisher twirled his thin moustache while he considered his next move.

"She'll do just fine," he sneered.

\* \* \* \* \* \* \* \* \* \*

Elizabeth Kendrick was waiting in the lobby when Bolt got there. She wore a bright red tailored shirt, tucked into black riding pants. Her blonde hair was pulled back away from her face, secured at the back of her head by a red ribbon. Small curls dangled at her forehead. She carried a wide-brimmed straw hat with a matching red ribbon.

"You look lovely, Miss Kendrick. Or may I call you Elizabeth?"

"Please call me Betsy."

"I like that better. Betsy."

They rode through the town, passed the false-fronts, then cut left at the edge of town.

"Where are we going?"

Bolt smiled at her, saw her large breasts bounce up and down beneath the material of her red blouse.

"Thought we'd see some of the country. There's a nice place over by the Smoky Hill River where we can have our picnic."

When the trail narrowed, Bolt took the lead. The horses threaded their way through boulders and scrub pines until they reached the place Bolt had picked out.

"You like it here?"

"Yes, it's beautiful. A perfect place for a picnic."

Bolt dismounted, helped her down off her mare. His hands brushed against firm breasts when he lifted her down. She flushed with the delicate pressure on her sensitive mounds, thought it was accidental.

"Jared, wouldn't it be fun to take our shoes off and wade in the river?"

"We got all afternoon. You hungry?"

"Starved."

He removed the saddlebags, flung them over his shoulder, then grabbed the blanket from behind the saddle. She helped him spread the blanket in the shade of a huge oak tree.

Betsy watched Bolt reach into a saddlebag, draw out a bottle. He unfastened the thongs of the other saddlebag and extracted a small bundle. She could smell the fried chicken. Bolt carefully unfolded the lumpy linen napkins and brought out two sparkling glasses. She watched in fascination as he opened the bottle, poured bubbly liquid into the two glasses. He handed one glass to Betsy, held the other up in a toast.

"To a lovely lady," he said, then clinked his glass to hers. "Why don't you call me Bolt, like everyone else. Jared's the handle my father tagged me with. I don't like it much."

"Bolt, I don't think I should drink this. My father never let me drink. Said it would get me in trouble, that nice girls didn't drink."

"Huh? It's just champagne."

"I guess a little won't hurt me." She eyed the glass tentatively then took a small sip. "It's good, but it tickles my nose."

Bolt laughed. They sat on the blanket, talking, sipping the champagne. Bolt found out that she was twenty-four and that she had lived with her over-protective father. Her mother died in childbirth and this was the first time she had been on her own. She was excited about teaching school. She didn't learn very much about Bolt because he let her do most of the talking.

A warm glow started in her stomach and spread to the rest of her body. She became more relaxed.

"You're a beautiful woman, Betsy," he said as he moved closer to her, poured another glass of champagne. When he put his arm around her, she didn't resist. He cupped his hand under her chin, squeezed her cheeks gently until her lips parted. He brought his mouth close to her, kissed her tenderly, his tongue darting into her open mouth.

She melted in his arms, felt the strange stirrings in her loins.

"Bolt, I feel so funny." She shuddered with excitement, tingled with desire.

"I want you, Betsy," Bolt husked as he tipped her back on the blanket, moved his hand down between her legs.

"We can't, Bolt. I . . . I've never done it before."

He wasn't surprised.

"I'll be very tender with you, Betsy. Let me take your clothes off. I'll make you feel good. I'll stop any time you tell me to."

He quickly removed her clothes, left her nude on the blanket while he undressed. She was fascinated by his erection, wanted to touch it, but was afraid to. He kissed her again, touched the large warm breasts with his hands, massaged them gently.

"You promise you'll stop when I say to?" she sighed. She was highly aroused by the feel of his warm body against hers.

"Yes, I promise. Your body is so smooth and beautiful, Betsy." He ran his hand over her bare, silken body. When he touched the bare flesh between her things, she shuddered. She didn't want to go all the way, but she wondered what it would feel like to have his swollen organ against her private parts.

"Bolt," she said hesitantly. "I want you to touch me down there with your . . . with it."

"Show me, Betsy," he urged, his voice cracking with desire. He took her hand and placed it on his swollen cock. Instinctively, she wrapped her hand around it, moved it up and down. She pulled the stiff organ over to her until it rested against her sensitive pussy lips. She felt an exquisite spasm as his manhood touched her.

She was confused. She wanted to stop Bolt and yet it felt so good to have his warm cock against her pussy lips. She wanted him to push against her, go in just a little bit.

"Push it in," she begged. "Just a little ways. Not all the way."

"Don't start anything you can't finish," he husked. "A man can't always stop when you want him to."

She didn't care. She had to have it inside.

"Do it to me, Bolt."

"Are you sure, Betsy?"

"I'm sure."

She thrust her pussy upwards.

# CHAPTER SIX

He rolled over on top of her, his precoital fluid leaving snail tracks on her bare thigh. He reached down and spread her lips, rubbed his slippery dampness across the portal. He lowered himself, touched her lips with his rigid member. She shuddered with pleasure. He pushed in slowly. She thrust her hips upward to meet him. He continued to push. Her maidenhead was thin and ruptured easily and painlessly with his gentle thrust.

He went deeper and deeper into her dark, damp cavern until she screamed with the ecstasy of orgasm. He paused, letting her enjoy the exquisite pleasure of the moment.

"Do you like it, Betsy?"

"Oh, yes. It feels so good. You're so big."

Her words fanned the fires in his loins. He plunged deeper, to the core of her sheath, into the steaming honey pot. Tight muscles gripped his swollen manhood, held it deep inside.

Bolt knew he could not hold back much longer. He stroked her slowly, deliberately, felt his sperm build. He plunged in again. Fireworks shot off in his brain as the spasms of orgasm convulsed through his body. He held Betsy tight until the spasms receded.

"You're very sweet," he said.

She wrapped her arms around his shoulders, pulled him close to her.

"Oh, I love you, Bolt. You're so good to me."

He moved off her, settled next to her on the blanket, a gentle breeze drying the love juices on his softening mass of flesh.

"Bolt?" she said in a soft voice.

"Yes?"

"I've never been in love before. I do love you. Very much. It's beautiful, isn't it?"

"Yes it is. And you're beautiful."

She looked over at Bolt in awe, as if he were some kind of god. He made her feel so wanted, so loved.

But a doubt existed. He hadn't said the words she wanted to hear. He hadn't told her he loved her. But he did, she was sure.

The sun was creeping low in the sky by the time they dressed and ate the food Tessie had prepared for them. They had talked and made love for hours.

"We'd better head back. It'll be dark in another hour," Bolt said.

As they crossed the shallow Smoky Hill River, they heard voices downstream. Bolt reined his horse to a halt. He looked down the river just in time to see a nude woman emerge from the chilly water. It was one of his girls, Annie. Climbing out of the water right behind her was an equally naked older man. The dripping couple tumbled onto a blanket.

Annie began manipulating the man's organ, took it into her mouth.

Betsy stared at the couple in shocked fascination. Her face flushed with embarrassment.

"Look at them, Bolt. They're doing it right out in front of everybody!"

"There's no one else around," Bolt laughed. "They're just enjoying the same thing we did a while ago."

"That's different. We did it in private."

Bolt shook his head. He'd never be able to understand the way a woman's mind worked.

Annie looked in their direction. Bolt hoped she hadn't seen them. He wouldn't like it if Annie told Cassie she'd seen him.

\* \* \* \* \* \* \* \* \* \*

The two men had done exactly as Chad Fisher had ordered.

They now held Cassie Owens hostage.

It had been easy as apple pie.

Once they knew for sure that Bolt was not at his whorehouse, Chad had explained his plan to lure the outlaw out in the open.

"We'll need a hideaway," Chad told them. "Someplace to keep his girlfriend until he comes after her."

"I know where there's an abandoned farm house," offered Bob Steckley. "It's about two miles from here. It's just a shack, really, but it'll do."

"Let's take a look at it. Atterbury, you stay here. Keep an eye on Bolt's place. I want to know if that bastard returns. We'll be back as soon as we check out the farm house."

He mounted his horse, let Steckley take the lead. They rode west, past the red light district where scantily dressed, painted girls hawked their wares from doorways and windowsills. A little beyond there, they took a road that angled off to the right. A mile and a half back in on the rough dirt road, they came upon the abandoned house.

"This used to belong to the Jensens when they first came to Abilene...."

"Don't matter," Fisher cut him off. "It's perfect. Set right out in the open. We got a clear field of fire in all directions. But he'll never make it this far. I'll cut him down before he gets here."

Big ugly rats scurried across the floor when the two men entered the weathered shack. A battered table tipped at a crazy angle, its broken leg beneath it. Four wobbly chairs sat around the broken table. Cardboard that had been tacked to the walls for insulation was peeling away, mute testimony to the heavy rains the year before. Two iron beds cradled stained mattresses that had chunks gouged out of them like half-eaten animal carcasses. Shreds of mattress and rat turds littered the floor. In a corner, the rat's nest, a heap of neatly shredded mattress particles, mixed with twigs and strips of rags.

On the counter top was a dusty coal oil lamp, black soot caked on the inside of the cracked chimney. A nearly full can of coal oil was on a shelf in the kitchen.

"This'll do. You can stay the night if you have to. Let's head back to town, get some grub before we kidnap the girl."

They ignored the taunts of the painted women when they rode back to town. Atterbury told them that Bolt hadn't returned to the bawdy house.

Chad mapped out his strategy while they ate supper at a small restaurant.

"We'll wait until late tonight before we make our move. Atterbury, I think you're the one to do the inside work. They might give Steckley a bad time if he goes back in there."

"What do you want me to do?" Atterbury asked.

"Go in, order a drink, keep your eyes and ears open. Find out where Cassie's room is. Once you're in there, you're on your own. But, between the two of you, I want Cassie. I'll give you a ransom note. Leave it with one of Bolt's employees. Tell him to give it to Bolt in the morning. I'll be waiting for him when he comes for his precious girlfriend."

When they finished eating, Fisher asked the waitress for a piece of paper and an envelope. When she returned, Chad wrote the message in his flourishing handwriting. He handed the note to Atterbury.

"See that this gets in the right hands. I'm going to head on out, make a dry camp somewhere near the road that leads out to the shack. Make sure you have some matches. You'll have to use that old lantern tonight. Take turns standing watch. And, don't mess around with the Owens girl! I don't want any distractions."

Atterbury entered Bolt's Bawdy House at 10 p.m. There was no sign of Bolt, nor his partner.

He walked over to the long bar, ordered a whiskey, removed his coonskin cap and set it on the bar. It wasn't long before he was approached by one of the glitter gals.

"Hello, good looking," said Ruby, her sensuous lips moist and inviting. She slithered onto the bar stool next to Atterbury.

"Can I buy you a drink?"

"Sure. I'll take champagne."

"Nice place you got here." He glanced around the room. That's when he spotted Cassie. He knew instinctively that the woman sitting at the end of the bar was Cassie Owens. She had too much class to be one of the ordinary glitter gals.

"Who's the pretty woman down there?" he asked, cocking his head in that direction. "She . . . she looks out of place."

"She's off limits," Ruby snapped. "She belongs to the boss."

"You mean Bolt?"

"Yeah. Do you know him?" Ruby fluffed her frizzy blonde hair, jutted out her large breasts that were barely covered by her scanty outfit.

"Not really. Only by reputation."

"Would you like a little fun while you're here?" Her hand slid over to his lap, squeezed his manhood.

"Sure." Hell, why not? Fisher hadn't said that he couldn't enjoy a little pleasure while he was there. Besides, he wanted to see the layout.

"Come on with me, lover boy," she husked, looping her arm through his. She led him upstairs where he paid her for a half hour's sexual favors. She gave him his money's worth and when he finally entered her, it was all over within a few short strokes. He was like an animal satisfying his own needs.

"You know, I'd like to own me a whorehouse. Where does Bolt sleep?" he said lamely, after they had dressed.

"He's got a room downstairs, by the back entrance."

"Where does his girl sleep?"

He had touched a sensitive area. All of the girls were a little jealous of Cassie.

"You mean when she's not sleeping with Bolt?"

"Yeah. Something like that."

"She has her own room, across from his."

"I'd like to see how this place is laid out downstairs. In case I ever get to build me one." He brought out a ten dollar bill from his pocket, handed it to her. "Something extra. You were good."

"Thanks. I'll show you around."

They walked down the hardwood stairway. Atterbury studied the large room below them as they descended. He saw the long bar taking up most of one side, the piano which was tinkling with music. Out of the corner of his eye, Atterbury could see that Cassie was still sitting at the bar.

Ruby led him down the hallway which was lit by lanterns hanging on the bare walls. She hesitated at the third door down the hallway. She pointed to the door on her left.

"This is Bolt's room. He keeps it locked." She walked a few more steps, reached for the handle of the door on the right. "Here's where Cassie lives."

She opened the door, let him look inside from the doorway.

"Fancy, isn't it?" she said.

"It's all right."

A dim ray of light shined through from the hallway. Atterbury couldn't see much, but he knew two things that would help him. Cassie's room was not locked and there was a window in it.

There was a door at the end of the short hallway. Atterbury walked to it, tried the handle. It was locked.

"What's in here?"

"That leads outside. The back door. We keep it locked. Nobody's allowed back here, down this hallway."

"Thanks for the tour. The place is bigger'n it looks."

"You're welcome," she said as they went back into the main room.

"Would you excuse me, Ruby. I want to get some fresh air." He had to get outside, talk to Steckley.

"Hurry back," she said coyly.

\* \* \* \* \* \* \* \* \* \*

"It took you long enough," said Steckley sarcastically. "Did you find out about Cassie and her room?"

"Yeah. I've got to get back in there. I want you to come inside, cause some sort of a diversion so that no one will see me go to her room. They don't let anybody down that hallway. Get in and get out fast. Just give me time to get to her room. When you get back outside, get our horses and bring them around back. Find her room and wait by the window." He explained the location of Cassie's room to the young boy.

Back inside, Atterbury went to the bar and handed a sealed envelope to Alec.

"Would you give this note to Bolt in the morning? Sorry I missed him."

A few minutes later, Bob Steckley came through the batwing doors. From her stool at the end of the bar, Cassie Owens saw the man stagger into the room. She recognized him immediately. Bob Steckley.

"Looks like he found a place to drink after he left here," she said to Alec. The bartender quickly moved from behind the bar. He made his way to the drunken troublemaker.

Only Steckley wasn't drunk. He was putting on a performance and hoped that everyone in the room was watching.

Steckley staggered to a table near the piano and plopped into a chair.

Atterbury was waiting. He made his move. He was sitting at a table near the back of the room, and when the other customers stood up to see what was going on, he stood with them, then slowly backed up toward the hallway.

Alec threaded his way through the customers.

Atterbury inched closer to the hall.

"You'll have to leave, Mr. Steckley," Alec said politely.

"Why? I just came to listen to the music," he slurred. "I ain't drinkin' here."

"You're drunk, Steckley. Now get out of here!"

Atterbury ducked into the hallway. He had it made now. Steckley's trick had worked.

"I ain't leaving. I got my rights," he said loudly.

Dan played the piano louder, trying to drown out the commotion. Alec grabbed Steckley by the arm and jerked him out of the chair.

The crowd gathered around, stretching their necks for a better view.

"You're on your way out. Now!" Alec said, pulling on the stubborn man. Steckley was dead weight as he stumbled against Alec. He flailed his arms in the air.

"I got rights! I just came to see the sissy play his piano."

Alec managed to get behind Steckley. He grabbed his arms, pulled them behind his back and pushed hard.

Dan jumped up from the piano stool.

"Hold him right there," Dan said. He doubled up his fist and let go, right in Steckley's stomach. "I owe you that one."

"Uuuuuugghh," moaned Steckley as the wind was knocked out of him.

Between Dan and Alec, they literally dragged Steckley to the batwing doors and pushed him hard. The young man tumbled down off the boardwalk, landed in the street.

"Don't ever come back!" Alec yelled. "Next time we won't be polite."

Will Atterbury laughed at the noise coming from the saloon. He was in Cassie's room. He struck a sulpher match against his pants, held it up for light. The match burned long enough for him to study the room, make his way to the double window. The flame burned his finger. He dropped the match to the floor after blowing it out. He made his way in the darkness to the window, tried to open it. It was locked. He felt around the window framing until he came to the lock on the sill. He released the lock, tugged at the window to open it.

The noise from the saloon died down. A couple minutes later, a ruffled Steckley appeared outside Cassie's bedroom window.

The customers in the saloon returned to their drinking, having something new to talk about.

"Think I'll retire early," Cassie told Alec. "I've had enough excitement for one evening."

## CHAPTER SEVEN

It wasn't the excitement of the encounter with a drunken Steckley that made Cassie tired. It was Bolt. She was worried about him. He had been gone all day, hadn't said where he was going. And she knew he had taken a box lunch for two. Alec told her that he took a bottle of champagne, too. It had to be another girl. Maybe not. He wasn't one to discuss his plans with her. It could be anything.

She glanced across the hall at Bolt's room when she went down the hallway. She couldn't help worry about him. She knew he was a hunted man.

She debated whether to go to his room and wait for him like she usually did. She didn't want him to think that she was trying to run his life or check on him. On the other hand, he always seemed to enjoy their lovemaking when he returned home late at night.

She made up her mind. She would go to Bolt's room and wait for him. She needed to be reassured tonight. First she would go to her room, wash up and get her nightgown.

She opened the door to her room, stepped inside.

She knew immediately that something was wrong.

She could smell the dead match. The sulphur scent that lingered in the air.

An arm swung around from behind her. A rough hand cupped over her mouth. Her scream froze in her throat before it had a chance to live.

Atterbury's other arm grabbed her around her thin waist. She felt something hard push against her midsection. She struggled to get free, kicked backward into thin air.

"Make one sound," said a gruff voice, "and you get this knife buried in your ribs." Atterbury jabbed at her for emphasis.

"Just move nice and easy over to the window." He nudged her from behind, kept the steel blade of the knife pointed at her back.

Cassie tried to open her mouth to bite his fingers. He clamped his hand tighter against her lips, forced them into her teeth. The pain was excruciating. She could taste the blood that oozed from the torn lining of her mouth.

When they reached the open window, he removed his right hand from her mouth and drew his pistol. She heard the click as he cocked the hammer back. He shoved her roughly through the open window frame into the arms of the man waiting outside. In the darkness, she couldn't tell who the arms belonged to.

"Get on your horse, Steckley. She'll ride behind you. I'll follow you. And don't get funny, lady. I got a pistol aimed at the back of your head. Any noise out of you and you're missing your pretty head."

Steckley mounted his horse, then helped Atterbury boost the girl up behind him.

"Wrap your arms around my waist and hang on," Steckley ordered.

Cassie did as he told her, cringing with repulsiveness.

Keeping the pistol leveled at her, Atterbury climbed atop his horse. The two men led their horses behind the buildings until they reached a point where they were well out of range of the bawdy house.

Fear crept into Cassie as the full impact of the kidnapping hit her. A stranger had been waiting for her in her room. But Bob Steckley was in on it. He wasn't drunk at all, she realized. That had been an act. But why? It had something to do with Bolt, she was sure. Maybe he'd been kidnapped, too. Or worse, maybe he'd been killed. Panic squeezed her heart, constricted her throat.

Ten minutes later, two horses passed by the place where Chad Fisher waited. He had set up a dry camp, was tucked back off the road, invisible to anyone passing by. He knew Atterbury and Steckley had been successful in their mission. He could see the outline of the two horses. The lead horse carried two passengers, one definitely a woman in a long, bulging dress. The second horse, with its solo rider, was close behind. It would not take them long to reach the hideout cabin.

Then the waiting would begin.

\* \* \* \* \* \* \* \* \* \*

It was late by the time Bolt got back to his place. He had gone up to Betsy's room and made love to her again. They had talked until way past midnight.

When he got to his room, he lit the lantern, removed his clothes and plopped in bed, contented and tired. He was relieved that Cassie wasn't there waiting for him, as she often was. He knew that Cassie was a jealous woman and he didn't want to face her after making love to Betsy.

\* \* \* \* \* \* \* \* \* \*

The next morning, Bolt woke, alert and refreshed. He washed up, dressed and went down for breakfast.

"Have you seen Cassie this morning?" he asked the bartender. "I want to talk to her."

"No, I haven't seen her yet. Funny, she's usually down here real early. Oh, by the way, I got a message for you. Some feller left it here last night."

Alec went over to the bar, came back holding an envelope.

"Who left it?"

"Don't know. Never seen the man before. He was a tall feller, mean looking. Wore a funny coonskin hat."

He grabbed the envelope from Alec, tore it open.

His blood froze in his veins.

He knew now why Cassie hadn't showed.

She had been kidnapped!

Bolt read the note again: "We have Cassie. If you want her back alive, bring $20,000 to the old Jensen cabin. Come alone. No tricks or she's dead." It was not signed.

He shook his head. He knew where the old Jensen cabin was. He'd gone by it yesterday when he was with Betsy.

"Was Atterbury alone?" Bolt asked.

"Who's Atterbury?"

"The man who gave you the note. The one who wore the coonskin cap. I'm willing to bet that it was Atterbury."

"I never saw the man before. He just came in and had a drink. Went upstairs with one of the girls. Ruby, I think. Then he handed me this note and asked me to give it to you this morning. Said he was sorry he missed you."

"I'll bet he was," said Bolt sarcastically.

Bolt dashed upstairs, knocked on Ruby's door.

A minute later, a sleepy, frizzle-haired blonde cracked her door open. "Who is it?"

"It's me, Ruby, Bolt. I have to talk to you a minute." She opened the door, let him in. Her large breasts jutted out above her nightgown.

"What's the matter?"

"I want to know about the man you entertained last night."

"Which one?"

"He wore a coonskin cap. Did he tell you his name?"

"He said it was Will. Didn't ask his last name. Why?"

"What did he do after he left you?"

"Well, he went outside to get some air."

"Did he come back in?"

"I don't know. I got busy with another customer. In fact I was up here with another gent when all that commotion was going on downstairs."

"What commotion?"

"That Steckley kid came in here drunk again. Tried to pick a fight with Dan, I think."

Bolt had some fast thinking to do. Cassie had been kidnapped. By that bastard Will Atterbury, he was sure. At least he had delivered the ransom note. But Atterbury wasn't the type to act alone.

He dashed to Cassie's room, opened the door. A breeze flapped the curtains at the open window. Everything else in the room seemed to be in order. The kidnapper had taken her out through the window. There hadn't been much of a struggle. Either they had knocked her unconscious or threatened her in some way.

Bolt met Tom Penrod in the hallway as Tom was coming out of his room.

"Cassie's been kidnapped," said Bolt.

"How? When?"

"I don't know yet. Sometime while I was gone last night. Were you here?"

"No. I got in late last night."

"I know that bastard Atterbury is in on it. I have a hunch that Bob Steckley was in on it, too. He was here last night. Drunk. But I think there's someone else, too. Just a feeling I got."

He shoved the ransom note to Penrod. "I don't think Atterbury or Steckley's educated well enough to have fancy writing like this."

"I don't think Steckley ever learned to read. What are you going to do? Take 'em the ransom money?"

"Hell no. It stinks like a trap. Stick around here. I may need you."

Bolt when to his room, picked up his binoculars, and headed for his horse outside. He knew a path to that old cabin that would keep him off the main dirt road that led to it. He didn't want to take any chances of another ambush.

He led the bay quietly through the brush and boulders, keeping his eye trained on the landscape so that he could detect any movement.

He pulled the reins up short when he spotted the old cabin. He was still a long way off, but he didn't want to risk going any closer just yet. He took the binoculars out of their case that dangled from his neck. His heart sank when he saw how barren the land was around the house. There was no easy access to it. No bushes or trees to hide behind. Just flat open country. He'd stand no chance if he rode straight in. He'd be cut down within three hundred yards of it if he tried it that way.

He couldn't detect any movement inside the cabin, even through the binoculars. But he was pretty sure there was someone there. A thin wisp of smoke came out of the chimney.

On the way back to his place, Bolt devised a plan. He would need Tom's help.

"Tom, I want you to do me a favor. Some risk."

"Yair. I'll bet."

"It's for Cassie, dammit. I wouldn't ask, otherwise."

"Yeah, I know."

"I want you to dress in my clothes, ride out to that abandoned cabin on my horse."

"Your horse?"

"My horse! Ride slow and go to within four to five hundred yards of the farmhouse. Don't go any closer. Stop the horse, dismount. Pretend you're studying the house real good. Then remount and ride in a slow circle all around it."

"What for? What'll you be doing?"

"It's better if you don't know. Just stay within that range. Act like you're kind of scared to go on in. They may show Cassie to you and I'm hoping they will. Maybe bring her out on the porch and threaten to kill her if you don't ride on in. Don't say a damned word."

"Sounds foolish to me."

"Do it."

Bolt went to his room, gathered up one of his outfits and handed it to Tom, who had followed him to his room.

"Now, get going," he told Tom. "Do exactly like I told you."

Bolt removed his boots, slipped into soft moccasins. He would wear no hat.

\* \* \* \* \* \* \* \* \* \*

Cassie huddled in one corner of the old shack, an old dusty blanket pulled close around her neck. The stench of rat droppings turned her stomach. Morning light filtered through the broken windows. She had not slept during the night. She was too frightened. Too cold, even though there had been a fire in the fireplace. She tried to think of ways to escape, but the two men had taken turns watching her. It was Steckley's turn now and she didn't like the way he was looking at her, his eyes all glittery and glazed over with lust.

"You and me could have some fun," he said, his voice cracking into a husk.

"Just keep your filthy hands off me," she glared. She hunched deeper into the blanket around her shoulders.

"You can't order me around, girlie. This ain't your place." He swaggered in her direction. She became sick to her stomach when she saw the bulge in his crotch tighten the material of his trousers. He reached for a breast, got an arm.

Will Atterbury walked through the doorway just at that moment.

"Steckley, you dumb bastard, get away from that girl. You know what Chad told us about that. He said we'd have plenty of time for messin' around with her after we get Bolt."

"Easy fer you to say. You got your rocks off last night with that hurdy-gurdy gal. Left me waitin' all the time while you was havin' yourself some fun."

"Knock it off, Steckley. It's time for you to stand watch outside anyway. Now get your ass out there."

Cassie was grateful for the big man's words. She couldn't stand having that dirty Steckley boy touch her, and the thought of him raping her was unbearable. She had learned a couple of things from the short conversation she overheard.

They were using her as bait to lure Bolt out in the open. She knew that for sure. And she knew that the man who had stopped Steckley from attacking her was called Atterbury. And there was another man. One they called Chad. One who seemed to be giving all the orders. One she had not seen.

She felt pretty sure that Atterbury was the man Bolt had told her about. The one who tried to ambush him and ran scared when Bolt had killed his cohorts. But she had ever heard Bolt mention the name Chad before.

\* \* \* \* \* \* \* \* \* \*

The lone gunman held his hand above his eyes, shading them from the morning sun. He scanned the countryside, watching for movement, for some sign of Bolt.

Chad Fisher had dozed briefly during the night, but kept an ear tuned for any noise, any sound that would signal Bolt's approach. Now he was getting nervous. Tension drew up the muscles in his shoulders, formed a knot at the back of his head. If he had it figured right, Bolt should be coming his way any minute now. He was about to score the biggest victory in his bounty hunting days.

Fisher paced back and forth, then sat under a tree. He leaned back against the trunk, gazed upward. A pair of hawks circled in the blue sky, searching for breakfast.

Yes, Bolt would be a big score for him, both moneywise and reputation wise. If Bolt brought the twenty grand, then that would all be gravy. He stood to collect two thousand bounty money and a thousand from Judge Wilkins. If he played his cards right, he had another thousand coming from that dumb-ass banker, Norvell.

"Twenty-five thousand," he said to himself. A man could live a while on that.

He stood up again and scanned the land. If Bolt didn't show soon, he'd go looking for him.

\* \* \* \* \* \* \* \* \* \*

Bolt left the Bawdy house shortly before Tom. He walked toward the abandoned farmhouse, staying just below the horizon. He chose a path that was well away from the road, kept his eyes and ears attuned to his surroundings.

He came over a rise, saw the shack a thousand yards away. He ducked down quickly, taking cover in the scrub brush. His tan trousers and shirt blended right into the dried bushes and grasses. He wore no hat because he didn't want to add anything extra to his silhouette. He had come up behind the house, a great distance away, and now he would have to make it the rest of the way without being detected if his plan was to work.

It would be tricky.

He crawled a short distance, then paused and looked toward the house. He saw no activity. He hoped Tom was where he was supposed to be. On his hands and knees, he inched a few more yards, stopped again. His movement was slow, deliberate, like a turtle. Damn, he wished he could rush the house, get it over with, be sure that Cassie was all right.

He crept another ten yards. The closer he got, the slower he went. A lizard darted across his path. His heart skipped a beat. Every little sound seemed magnified in his ears. When he got to within two hundred yards of the house, he stretched out flat on the ground and pulled himself along the ground with his elbows. He moved first one elbow forward, then the other one. Then, with all his effort, he pulled his body forward, like an inch worm.

A fly landed on his face, crawled around and settled on his nose. He didn't dare move an arm up to swat it away. He blew at it with his lower lip. It hopped off his nose, buzzed at his ears. Perspiration trickled down his forehead, splashed into his eyes. The salt stung his eyeballs. He blinked it away.

Time ticked away. An inch. A minute. Another inch. Another minute.

When he was twenty-five feet away, he heard a man yell.

"There he is! I can see him!" screamed the excited man.

"Shit!" thought Bolt. "They've spotted me."

## CHAPTER EIGHT

Bolt froze.

It was a moment before he realized that they were talking about Tom.

"Yeah, that's him. That's Bolt," yelled Steckley. "That's his horse."

Bolt recognized Steckley's whiney voice. His hunch was right. Steckley was in on this kidnap. Now if his other hunch was right, there would be three men inside that cabin instead of two.

He pulled himself along through the dusty earth toward the house. His elbows ached from the small pebbles that gouged at his skin. He could see blood staining the shirt sleeves that were torn through at the elbows. Only a few more feet to go.

He crawled to a blind corner of the shack, stood up, pressing his body in tight against the building. He could make out two distinct voices coming from inside the house.

"Why don't that bastard Bolt ride up here like he's supposed to?" said an angry Steckley.

" 'Cause Bolt don't always do what he's s'posed to!" yelled Atterbury.

"Look at that chicken shit. He acts like he's scared to come on in," said Steckley. "He's just ridin' around out there. Wait! He's gettin' off his horse. Now he's lookin' this way."

Atterbury hunched down in front of the open window, his rifle aimed at the figure beside the horse. Steckley kept his pistol on Cassie, stretching behind Atterbury to see what he could.

"He's back on his horse," said Atterbury. "I think he's comin' now."

"Come on, man," Steckley said. "We're waiting for ya!" He said this in a low voice, much like a dice player would speak to the die.

"Hell, he's not coming in," said Atterbury disgusted. "I'm going to try a long shot. I think I can take him out from here."

Cassie started to get up from her corner. She wanted to warn Bolt.

"Stay right where you are, girlie," warned Steckley. He waved his pistol menacingly in her direction. Then he turned to Atterbury. "Don't shoot yet. He's too far away to get a good shot at him. We don't dare mess up. We'll just wait him out. He'll come after his galfriend sooner or later."

"Damn," said Atterbury. "If he just comes a little closer, I know I could get him."

The minutes ticked by as Tom rode Bolt's horse back and forth, keeping his distance from the old shack. He felt silly, but figured Bolt had his reasons.

"I've got an idea," said Atterbury. "It just might work. Bring that gal over here. Maybe Bolt don't believe we got her here. We'll show him the real live thing. Use her as bait. We'll take her outside and once Bolt gets a glimpse of her, he won't waste no time gettin' here. You can bet your sweet ass on that."

Steckley jerked her roughly to her feet, dragged her over to where Atterbury was standing.

"Now," said Atterbury, "we're going through that front door nice and easy. Keep your pistol right up snug against her temple. Make sure Bolt can see it. Come on, let's go."

Tom Penrod saw the three figures appear on the front porch. He knew the woman was Cassie and he didn't miss the pistol that was shoved against her head. Shit, what was Bolt up to? He didn't even know where Bolt was. He felt helpless. He had promised Bolt that he would stay his distance, not speak at all.

"You comin' after your girl, Bolt?" Atterbury called. The trio moved out a little father so they could be easily seen.

That's just what Bolt was waiting for.

He made his move. Dashing to the back of the house, he crawled in a back window. He planned to come up behind the gunmen, catch them off guard. But then the oil lantern caught his eye, gave him a better idea.

He grabbed the lamp, tipped it over and spilled the coal oil all over the floor. He sprinkled some of the fluid on the furniture, the curtains. He snatched the sulphur matches from the counter top, struck one and touched it to the curtains in the back of the room. He jumped out the other back window and stalked around to the front.

"Drop it right there," he yelled.

The startled gunmen jerked their heads toward Bolt's voice. They stood there staring at him, slack-jawed. Atterbury did a double take, looking at the distant rider he thought was Bolt and then back at the real thing. Obediently, he lowered his rifle, dropped it gently to the porch.

Steckley watched Atterbury, then followed his lead, leaning down to place his pistol on the weathered slats of the porch. His left hand still gripped the frightened girl's arm.

"Come here, Cassie," Bolt called.

She wrestled free of Steckley's grasp and dashed to Bolt.

"Thank God you're here," she said, trembling. "What do we do now?"

"We run like hell!" He grabbed her hand, dragged her behind him. She stumbled over a rock, flailed her arms in the air to regain her balance.

The two men stood motionless for a moment, dumbfounded by the turn of events. They recovered quickly and reached for their weapons, began firing at the fleeing couple.

Wild shots poured after Bolt and Cassie as they zigzagged across the open field, away from the house.

Tom Penrod saw what was happening. He drew his pistol, kicked Bolt's horse in the flanks and charged toward the house. He fired one shot. It whizzed over the heads of the two gunmen. His second shot, at closer range, grazed Steckley's arm.

"Holy shit!" screamed Steckley.

"Back in the house! Quick!" yelled Atterbury. He ducked and dashed into the house, Steckley right behind him.

Flames lapped at the walls of the old shack, burned a path across the decaying floor. Steckley's eyes widened in horror. The two men turned around, started to go back outside. They got to the doorway. Penrod was right outside, ready to nail them. One shot. Then another from Penrod's pistol drove them back inside. They huddled near the doorway.

The room was filled with leaping flames and black, choking smoke. The heat was intense.

"We gotta get out of here quick, or we're gonna fry," yelled Steckley, gasping for breath.

Atterbury grabbed a handkerchief from his pocket, cupped it over his nose and mouth. He looked for an escape exit.

"There's only one way out," he said, his voice raspy from the smoke. "Make a dash for it! Out the back window!"

Atterbury made a run for it. A chunk of floor burned through, gave way before him. He dodged the gapping hole it left, knocked over a flaming chair. Angry flames licked at him. He spurted to the charred window frame, leaped through it, landed on the hard ground.

Bob Steckley huddled near the front door a moment longer. He was too frightened to dash through the flames. He saw his partner disappear into the inferno. He didn't know if Atterbury had made it or not. He knew he would be cut down by a bullet if he tried to run out the front way. Finally, he gritted his teeth, held his breath, and plunged into the billowing smoke. Flames reached out for him from all directions. He tripped over the chair that Atterbury had knocked over. He fell flat on his face on the floor, which probably saved his life. A flaming beam crashed down right where he would have been if he hadn't tripped. His trousers caught fire, around his ankle. He jumped up, leaped high in the air, over the fallen beam. He saw the window frame amid the drifting smoke. In one final effort, he managed to throw himself through the open space. He landed with a thump. Pain sored through his leg as the flame ate through his pat leg. He started slapping at the flame, which fanned it.

"Roll over on the ground, you asshole!" yelled Atterbury when he saw the burning clothing, He ran over to Steckley and scooped up loose dirt with his hands, tossed it on the man's leg. Steckley helped him, digging his own hands into the earth and heaping the dirt on top of the wounded leg. The fire died out, smothered.

"You all right?" Atterbury asked.

"Yeah, I think so," said the shaken youth.

When the front of the shack went up in flames, Tom knew it was time to go. He had served his purpose by providing the cover Bolt and Cassie needed to get away. He had seen them disappear over the rise a few minutes before, knew they were safe. He didn't know about the men inside the burning cabin, didn't care. He turned Bolt's horse around, kicked it to a gallop, headed for home the shortest way he knew.

\* \* \* \* \* \* \* \* \* \*

Was that gunfire? Chad Fisher couldn't be sure. He heard four or five little pops. There it was again, two more slight cracks. Could be someone hunting. He got up from the tree he had been leaning against, scanned the landscape again. He took off his hat, ran his fingers through his straight dark hair. He rubbed the back of his head, trying to get rid of the tension. He had been waiting a long time for Bolt to show up. He should have ridden by a long time ago on his way to get Cassie Owens back. He had learned a lot about Bolt, and one of those things was that he protected his women. He had heard that Bolt never bought his women, but that he treated his whores like respectable ladies. He also knew that the females were attracted to Bolt for some reason. Maybe he'd find out why.

He thought about the first man he had hunted down and killed. Benny Larson. The bastard had killed Chad's best friend, shot him in the back. The townspeople had raised bounty money. He would have gone after the killer anyway, but the bounty was an added bonus, and when he got the killer, he became a hero. He gloried in the attention he got. He had gone after other outlaws for bounty money, and he always got his man.

He had gained a reputation in the West. He was often called in on rough assignments when others failed to do the job. And he always delivered. Dead or alive. Whatever they wanted.

He had a motto: The bigger they are, the harder they fall.

Well, Bolt was in for a mighty hard fall.

There was that noise again. Two little pops. It had to be gunfire. That was the only thing it could be.

He wouldn't wait any longer. His patience was exhausted. Maybe Bolt had gone to the cabin a different way.

He mounted his horse, kicked him in the flanks. He pulled on the reins and the horse headed north. He would go to the cabin first, check with the boys. The road curved around through a swampy area, then came out in the flat.

That's when he saw the billow of smoke in the distance. He whipped the horse with the reins. The horse sped toward the cabin.

Chad was sick when he saw the burning farmhouse. Anger began to boil deep inside him.

Steckley and Atterbury looked up and saw Fisher approaching. They walked toward him, glad that he was there to tell them what to do next. Steckley limped, favoring the leg that was burned. The wound was raw and ugly, oozing fluid, and it hurt like hell. But he was lucky. The burned area was fairly small, about the size of a palm. It could have been worse. It could have been fatal.

"What happened here? Where's the girl?" Fisher asked.

"Bolt tricked us," offered Atterbury. "He used a decoy, that partner of his, and he snuck up behind us. Set the house afire."

"Yeah," said Steckley, "and he got the gal away from us."

"You mean to tell me that you just let Bolt walk up here and take his girlfriend, burn the house down? What were you doing all this time? Beating off?"

"But, he tricked. . . ." Steckley started.

"I don't want any of your fuckin' excuses," said Fisher. "You blew your chance. You're a couple of chicken shit cowards!"

"But it wasn't our fault," said Will. "It all happened so fast."

"Who in hell's fault was it, you dumb bastards? Where are your horses? Or did he get those, too?"

"No," said Atterbury, "we hid our horses out, way up beyond the house."

Chad noticed the raw wound on Steckley's leg.

"Looks mighty bad," he said. "You got burned, didn't you?"

"Yes," said a sheepish Steckley.

"Will, go get the horses. Bring them back here. We got some tracking to do. Bolt'll be on guard now. Damn, we gotta get him. He may come lookin' for us."

"We can go to my ranch," offered Steckley. "Give us a chance to figger out our next move."

"Might not be a bad idea. Bolt will be extra careful right now. Give him a chance to let his guard down."

Steckley sat down on the ground to take the weight off his leg. Atterbury left to retrieve the stashed horses. Chad looked at the collapsed remains of the farmhouse. There wasn't much left of it. Small flames ate away at the pile of logs. The smoke would linger a long time.

Chad was madder than hell that Steckley and Atterbury had missed their chance to get Bolt.

He was furious that Bolt and his girl had gotten away and there was no big ransom money.

Most of all, he was angry at himself — for being outsmarted by Bolt.

Now, he would just kill him. The money didn't matter anymore. It was a grudge fight now.

He hated to be outsmarted.

And, he had a reputation to uphold.

He always got his man.

## CHAPTER NINE

They were out of breath by the time they reached the river. Cassie sagged to the ground, panting. Bolt sat down next to her, put his arm around her shoulders. Her body began to tremble.

"It's all right now, Cassie," he said tenderly. "It's over with."

She began to weep.

"Oh, Bolt, I was so frightened. I thought they were going to kill you. I thought they might kill me. And that Steckley boy, he was going to . . . he tried. . . ."

"Did he do anything to you?"

"No, but he was going to."

"Calm down, Cassie. You're safe now." He pulled her close to him. "Was there anyone else besides those two gunnies, Steckley and Atterbury?"

"I only saw the two of them. Steckley was in the saloon last night causing trouble. Alec and Dan tossed him out. But I didn't know the other fellow — the one who was waiting in my room. His first name's Will. I heard Bob call him that."

"Atterbury. I've had a run-in with him before."

"But someone else was giving the orders, I know."

"Who?"

"I don't know. I never saw him. I heard them talking about someone called Chad. He was the one who told them what to do. I got that much from their conversations."

"It figures."

"Bolt, I wish we could get married. I want to be with you all the time. I need you. I feel safe when I'm with you."

"I'm the one who's being tracked. You're better off without me. You're fine now. We'd better get going. Get back home. Can you make it?"

"Yes. I'm all right."

He rose, helped her up. He looked at her.

"You're beautiful, Cassie. Even with your dirty face," he teased.

She ran a hand across her cheek, fluffed her dirty, rumpled dress.

"I know. I must be a sight." She smiled at him, locked her arm through his.

\* \* \* \* \* \* \* \* \* \*

Alec set the two whiskies on the table, walked back to the bar.

"It's so nice to have you around all the time, Bolt," Cassie smiled. "It's been a week since you've left this place."

"Yeah, I know." Bolt's face was dark. He had kept a low profile, staying at his bawdy house. It was beginning to eat at him. He was not a man to be trapped in his own place.

"Bolt, what's the matter?"

"I dunno. Just restless, I guess." He knew what the matter was, but didn't want to tell her. She had followed him around like a puppy for a couple of days, hinted at marriage more times than he cared to remember. He didn't need that kind of pressure. Not now. Not anytime.

Cassie wasn't the real problem anyway, he knew. It was the man who stalked him. The man called Chad. He wished Cassie could give him a description or a last name. Anything. But she couldn't.

It was unnerving to know that someone was waiting out there somewhere to snuff his candle. It made him irritable, overcautious.

Every stranger who stepped through the doors of his establishment was a potential threat to Bolt, as far as he was concerned. At least that was the way he had felt the past week. He eyed every man suspiciously, studied his mannerisms, paid special attention to his eyes. He had the ability to size up a man in a hurry. He had to. It had become second nature to him. He didn't want to be caught off guard.

"Cassie?"

"Yes?"

"I talked to Tom this afternoon. We're going over to Dodge City to look at some ranch properties."

"When you going?" She looked down, a darkness clouding her face.

"In the morning."

She shot him a look, searched his eyes for some explanation.

"So soon?" She fought back the tears that welled up. She felt she was losing him. She wanted desperately to go with him. But she wouldn't ask. Bolt was not a man to be tied down. She realized that she had to accept him for what he was, enjoy him while she could.

\* \* \* \* \* \* \* \* \* \*

Betsy answered the knock at her door, hoping it was Bolt. She hadn't seen him since the day they went picknicking. The day she gave her heart and virginity away. She was beginning to have self doubts. At times she thought that maybe she hadn't pleased Bolt. But then, she reasoned, she had been busy herself getting the new school term under way.

She opened the door a crack, peeked out. Her eyes widened with surprise and she smiled. She flung the door open.

"Father, what a surprise. What are you doing here?"

"On my way to Colorado. Thought I'd stop and see how my little girl is doing."

"I'm not a little girl, Father. Come on in." She eyed him suspiciously for a moment. "I hope you're not checking up on me."

"No, just passing through."

She knew better than that. Her father was always checking up on her. That's one of the reasons she had taken the teaching job so far from home. To get out from under the constant scrutiny of her over-protective father.

Over coffee, she told him all about her job as school marm, about the children, the things she was teaching them.

"Father, I think I'm in love," she blurted out. She could have bitten her tongue. She hadn't meant to tell her father about her personal life. It just popped out. It was something she thought about all the time, even when she was at school.

"Oh?" He cocked a suspicious eyebrow.

"Well, ah, yes. I met this man, and uh . . . well, he's the nicest man. . . ."

"What's his name?"

"Jared Bolt. Oh, Father, you'd love him."

"What does he do?"

"I, uh, I don't know."

Her father knew. Anger boiled inside him, flushed upward, colored his face red. He knew who Bolt was. He had read the posters in towns he passed through. And, he had stopped at Bolt's Bawdy House on the way in to Abilene. Oh, yes, he knew who Bolt was.

"Do you know anything about him?"

"Yes, I know him," she stammered. She realized that she didn't really know anything about the man she loved. Only that he was a good man; a gentle, loving man. She knew how she felt about him.

Something in her father's voice alarmed her. But then that was normal. Her father had never liked any of the boys she had dated, which weren't many. He always interferred, told her they weren't good enough for her.

"Did you. . . . Did he, ah make advanced to you?"

Her face blushed crimson. Could her father tell that by looking at her? Did it show when a woman had been made love to? She didn't care any more. She knew she was in love with Bolt.

"Yes."

He kept a calm exterior, but inside he was fuming with rage.

"I'll tell you who your boyfriend is. He's an outlaw. A criminal. And, he owns his own whorehouse." He punctuated the last statement.

"I don't believe you! You're lying to me! You always say something bad about the boys I like!" She was incredulous. She wouldn't believe those things about Bolt.

"It's the truth, Betsy. Believe me. I've heard about him. He's a murderer, a bank robber."

"He couldn't be!"

"His whorehouse is right here in Abilene. I stopped at the saloon and had a quick drink on my way here." He didn't tell her that he had also bought the services of one of the girls.

"I've never seen it. Never even heard of it." She clung desperately to her beliefs that Bolt was a good man, a decent, honest man.

"He used you, Betsy. Used your body for his own pleasure, just like you was some cheap, filthy whore!"

The words bit into her, tore at her core of decency. She began to weep as waves of humiliation washed over her. She sobbed uncontrollably, hating herself for what she had done with Bolt. How could anything so beautiful turn out to be so sordid? Now she understood why he had a box of new sheets in the buckboard at the train station.

Suddenly her humiliation turned to anger.

"Father, take me to . . . take me to his place! I want to see for myself!"

\* \* \* \* \* \* \* \* \* \*

Bolt saw the tears welling up in Cassie's eyes. He felt a sudden tenderness toward her. She was a good woman. A damned good woman. Why did women have to get so attached to a man? He guessed he'd never understand how a woman felt. He reached out, placed his hand on hers.

"Yes, Cassie, I have to go tomorrow. You'll be safe here. Safer than you'd be with me. Besides. . . ."

His eyes automatically went to the batwing doors as they creaked open. His mouth fell open, mid-sentence. What in the hell was Betsy Kendrick doing here? He saw her push her way through the doors, pause and look around. Behind her was a tall whip-lean, almost cadaverous-looking man with a hard look in his eyes. What the hell was going on?

Betsy spotted him, stormed straight for him.

Bolt rose from his chair as the angry girl approached him. Betsy pulled her arm back and slapped him hard across the face. Bolt stood there, astonished.

"You louse!" she shouted. "You . . . you no good. . . ."

She drew her arm back again, swung and missed. Bolt ducked.

"Hey, wait a minute!"

She flailed her arms in the air, wanting to tear his hair out, wanting to scratch his eyeballs blind.

"So it's true! What my father told me about you!"

Bolt glanced beyond her, at the man glaring at him. He saw the family resemblance.

Betsy turned hysterical. She pounded on Bolt's chest with tiny fists. Bolt started to reach for her wrists, changed his mind when he saw the deadly look in her father's eyes. The older man watched every move, never said a word.

Cassie jumped up, got behind Betsy and grabbed her by the shoulders. She didn't know who this frantic girl was, but she had a pretty good idea. A woman scorned.

Betsy turned, flung her arms wildly at Cassie.

"You must be one of his stinking whores!" screamed Betsy. She yanked at Cassie's head, came up with a handful of dark shiny hair. She dug sharp fingernails into Cassie's arm, raked them through the soft flesh. Cassie slapped the girl on the cheek, trying to bring her out of her hysterics.

Tom Penrod hopped off his barstool. He was joined by Alec, who came around the end of the bar. Together, they managed to pull the two women apart.

Kendrick grabbed his daughter's hand.

"Come on, I'm taking you back home before somebody dies real sudden."

The father and daughter were gone as quickly as they appeared.

"Who was she?" Cassie asked, glancing down at her arm. Blood trickled from four long gouges.

"Just a friend."

"Hmph. Some friend!" she snorted as she huffed off.

"You can sure pick 'em," Tom kidded. "She was some little wildcat, that one."

"Yeah," said Bolt. "She was madder'n a wet hornet. But did you see her father? Kendrick is some kind of mean. I had the feeling he was going to draw, if I made one wrong move."

"I told you a woman would get you in trouble some day. Hell, women are always gettin' you in trouble. When're you gonna learn to pay for your women like I do? Save you a lot of agony."

" 'Cause I don't believe in paying for it," said Bolt.

"Hell, you don't see a swarm of angry husbands and fathers after me, do you?"

"Makes it more interesting this way," Bolt smiled. "You ought to try it sometime."

\* \* \* \* \* \* \* \* \* \*

It was almost noon when they reached the Saline River. If they held their pace, they'd reach Ellsworth before dark.

Bolt and Penrod had left Abilene long before sunrise.

Cassie was still asleep when he left that morning, in his bed. She had asked if she could sleep with him on their last night together. He had chided her, told her it wasn't the end of the world, that he would be back. Their lovemaking had been sweet.

Sweat trickled down Bolt's forehead, stained the armpits of his shirt. Tom looked up at the high noon sun, wiped an arm across his brow. It was a blistering day for September.

Bolt dipped his hat into the river, caught water in it, and dumped it on his head.

Something across the river caught Bolt's eye. Some slight movement in the clump of trees. Five hundred yards away. Low. Near the ground. His skin began to tingle. The hairs on the back of his neck bristled.

"Tom," he said in a whisper.

"Yeah?"

"Look over at those trees. See anything?"

Tom peered across the river.

"Nope. Just the trees."

"I saw something move."

"Probably an animal. Rabbit or coyote."

"Yeah, maybe. But I got an eerie feeling. Had it for the past couple of hours. Like someone's following us."

"Bolt, you're as jumpy as a cat in a room full of rocking chairs. Relax."

Bolt let the horses drink their fill at the river and then turned to Tom.

"Come on, let's get out of here. I have a feeling someone's breathing down our necks. I can feel it in my bones. I can even smell it."

\* \* \* \* \* \* \* \* \* \*

The young man sprawled motionless on the ground until Bolt and Penrod mounted their horses and rode away. When they had rounded a bend in the road, he rose and scampered up a slope. He disappeared beyond a rise.

Waiting for him were Chad Fisher and Will Atterbury.

"That gal was right," panted Bob Steckley. "They're headed for Ellsworth. I know this territory like the back of my hand. Used to herd cattle out this way. I know a shortcut to Ellsworth. It's rough country, but we can beat them there by an hour."

## CHAPTER TEN

It was two hours past sunset when they saw the twinkling lights of Ellsworth up ahead. It had been too hot during the afternoon to keep the horses going at the pace Bolt wanted. They had stopped often to let the horses rest.

"Guess you were right, Tom."

" 'Bout what?"

"About me being jumpy. I could have sworn that someone was on our tail, though. At least this morning. Guess there's no use looking for trouble."

They cut off to the right just before they got to the small town. It was the road that led to Bolt's father's home. It was the first time Bolt had been home since he had left five years before. Tom didn't care if he never saw Ellsworth again.

Bolt's father heard the horses approaching and was on the porch when they rode up, a lantern in his hand.

"Thank God you're here, Jared," he said. "Your brother's been shot!"

Bolt dismounted quickly, tied his horse to the porch rail.

"How bad's he hurt?"

"Not too bad. They got him in his left arm. The bullet went clean through. The doctor left a while ago. He cleaned the wound. Wrapped it up. Michael's resting now."

"Who shot him?" Bolt asked.

"He doesn't know. He didn't see anyone. The shot came from the direction of the stables. He and his friend, Joe Bainbridge, were riding home. Someone was waiting for him. I heard the shot and ran outside, but I didn't see nobody. Twas getting near dark. Joe went right away fer the doc."

The hairs on the back of Bolt's neck began to bristle again. A cold ball of steel formed in his stomach.

"I don't think that bullet was meant for Michael, Father."

"What do you mean, Jared?"

"I think it had my name on it." He shook his head and went inside.

Michael looked over from his bed when Jared walked in. His eyes were glazed over, partly from shock and partly from the whiskey the doctor had given him to ease the pain.

"How are you feeling?" asked Bolt.

"Not too bad," said Michael.

"The doctor said Michael was to rest, Jared, so don't talk too long," the preacher said from the bedroom doorway. "Come on, Tom, I'll make some coffee." He turned and went to the kitchen. Tom followed him.

"You don't know who shot you?" Bolt said.

"No. I never saw him. It was almost dark."

"I know. Father told me. Michael?"

"Yes."

"I feel real bad about you taking that bullet. I'm sure it was meant for me. I think someone was following us here. They just beat us here, mistook you for me."

"I don't know," said Michael. His speech was slurred, his eyes heavy-lidded. He looked up at his brother, a sad look on his face. Suddenly, he began to sob uncontrollably. His wide shoulders bucked with anguish.

"What's the matter, Michael? Is the pain that bad?"

"No. It . . . it's not the . . . the pain," he sobbed. "Jared, God is punishing me. I just know He is."

"Why would you say that? You ain't done nothing."

Bolt had seen men do this before when whiskey fuzzed over their thinking. Whiskey was funny that way. It kind of scrambled the brains up. Some men got real ornery when they drank. They talked tough, acted real mean. He'd seen men try to take on a whole saloon full of men, feeling tall and strong. But, he'd seen a man get on a crying jag, too, like Michael was doing now. Sometimes guilt or self pity, whether it be real or imagined, came pouring out from thick tongues. Babbling.

"No, Jared. I've sinned. Sinned real bad."

"You don't know what you're sayin', Michael. You're talkin' out of your head. You get some sleep and we'll talk in the morning. You'll feel better then." Jared turned, started to walk away.

"No, Jared. Wait . . . please listen to me."

"O.K., Michael. Go ahead." Bolt pulled a wooden chair over near the bed and sat down. He crossed his arms on his knees, leaned forward.

"It's about . . . about Amy. Amy Robinson. And her little boy."

Bolt sat up straight, leaned back.

"I don't want to hear any more about poor Amy and about her poor little boy. That's all you and Father ever talk about. I'll be damned if I'm going to sit here and listen to you lecture me about morals and my responsibility to Amy. She. . . ."

"Jared," Michael interrupted. "Hear me out. It's me. It's me!"

"What are you talking about?"

"I'm the father of Amy's child!" Michael blurted. "Not you!" He wept openly, shivering with anguish.

Bolt was stunned. He didn't know what to make of it. He wondered if this was just more drunk talk.

"Say it plain and straight, Michael."

"I've known it all these years. I'm some ashamed. That little boy is mine. I knew it even before you and Amy . . . even before you. . . . That's why I chased you all those years . . . tried to get you to come home and marry Amy."

"Easy, Michael." Jared reached over and patted his brother on the shoulder. "You're not making much sense."

"Amy and I were in love once, five or six years ago. I still love her. We used to go for secret walks, pretend we were on our own. We fooled around a little. Never did anything but kiss and hug and feel each other. But one day I got . . . I got so excited that we . . . I talked her into going all the way. It was my fault. I told her if she loved me, she'd let me do it to her. I know you don't understand, Jared, but that day I just couldn't control myself. I thought I'd burst if I didn't have her."

"I understand, Michael." Jared felt compassion for his brother. For all these years Michael had been weighted down with guilt because he had followed a basic urge.

"After that first time," Michael continued, "we did it whenever we could. We planned ways we could be together. We talked about getting married some day and having children. Then that one day, the day she told me she was expecting a baby. I got scared. Real scared. I knew people would find out about it. I knew Father would be ashamed of me. I didn't know what he'd do to me."

"He'd have forgiven you, Michael," Jared said softly.

"I'm not so sure. I thought so for a while, but then I know he never forgave you when he thought you were the father. I was so confused. I told Amy I wouldn't marry her. I stayed away from her, wouldn't talk to her. That's when she went after you. She told me she'd get even with me and I guess she thought if she did it with you, it would hurt me. Then Father caught the two of you in the hay loft that day. After you left town, she came begging me to marry her again. I wanted to but I was confused. It hurt me when you and she. . . . Anyway, that's why I followed you all those years.

I just couldn't face Amy after she had the baby. I couldn't face Father or the townspeople. It was easier to blame you and stay away from here."

"Do you still love Amy?"

"Yes, I do. After I saw you that time in Fort Scott, I came back home. When I saw Amy and that sweet little boy, I knew I loved them both. I see them a lot now."

"Does Amy know how you feel? Have you ever asked her to marry you?"

"No. I've wanted to, but I never have."

"Why, Michael?"

"I guess I figured she was still mad at me because I didn't marry her when she found out about the baby."

"Does Amy love you?"

"I don't know. Sometimes, when she looks at me with those sad eyes, I think maybe she does."

"Do you want to marry her, live with her the rest of your life?"

"Yes, but I don't know if she'd marry me after I turned her away like I did."

"No way of knowing unless you ask."

"I don't know what people would think...."

"The devil with what people think. This is between you and Amy. It's your lives. That's what counts. People in this town don't need to know anything but what you want to tell them."

"Maybe you're right."

"You'd better get some sleep now. I'll be here for a day or two. Talk to you in the morning." The chair scraped against the wooden floor as Bolt stood up.

"How's he feeling?" asked Elijah when Jared walked into the kitchen.

"He's feeling much better, I'm sure," smiled Bolt.

"I'm going to town, Bolt," said Tom. "Want to come along?"

"No thanks. I'll stay here. I'll walk out with you. Put my horse up."

"Be careful out there," his father warned.

"I think we got trouble here in Ellsworth," Bolt said when they were outside.

"Whatdya mean?" asked Tom.

"I'm pretty sure that whoever shot Michael was waiting for us to show. It was dark enough when it happened so they might make that mistake. And I've got a hunch that it was those three that kidnapped Cassie: Steckley, Atterbury and the one they call Chad."

"Doesn't make sense, Bolt."

"Tom, Michael doesn't have an enemy in the world. I talked to him about that. Nobody would be shootin' at him."

"Just a coincidence, Bolt. Your Pa said that Michael was shot two hours before we got here. Couldn't have been anyone following us. How in the hell would they know we were coming to Ellsworth?"

"That's what bothers me."

\* \* \* \* \* \* \* \* \* \*

The horse and buggy was parked in front of Preacher Bolt's house when Jared returned from town the following afternoon. He hoped Michael hadn't taken a turn for the worse. His trip to town had proved futile. There was no sign of any of the men he was looking for. He had talked to Tom while he was in town. He hadn't seen the men either.

Bolt dismounted quickly, tied his horse to the hitch rail. He looked at restless horses that were hooked to the buggy, then went inside.

He immediately recognized the voice that floated out from Michael's bedroom. He hadn't heard it for over five years.

Bolt took his hat off, walked into the livingroom where his father was sitting. He sat on the couch, balanced his hat on his knees.

"Amy's here, Jared," Elijah said. "She heard about Michael and came to visit him."

"I know, Father. I heard her voice when I came in."

"She brought your . . . her little boy with her. He's the spittin' image of you. I hope you'll marry. . . ."

The door to Michael's bedroom opened.

He heard the footsteps on the hardwood floor. Light delicate steps mixed with the scuffle of a youngster's shoes. Heavier steps following those.

He looked up as she entered the room, saw a beautiful woman standing there. She was tall and slim now, with graceful curves. Bolt had remembered her as chubby and freckle-faced, aggressive and domineering. She looked older, more matronly with her dark red hair tied in a bun behind her head. Her brown eyes had a twinkle to them as she extended a delicate hand. Michael stood beside her, his bandaged arm in a sling.

"Hello, Jared." She smiled, exposing white even teeth. "It's so good to see you again."

"The pleasure's mine," he said as he shook her hand.

She reached down and put her hands on the shoulders of the young boy who clung shyly to her long skirt.

"This is my son, little Joe."

Bolt stooped down, one knee on the floor, and stuck his hand out to the boy. The little boy looked at him, then lowered his head, hiding it in the folds of his mother's skirt. Elijah had been right. The lad looked like a Bolt with his dark eyes and brown hair. The family resemblance was there. Jared stood up again and gestured toward the couch.

"Have a seat," he said to Amy. He felt awkward offering Amy a seat. After all, she had spent a lot more time in this house than he had recently.

"How are you feeling, Michael?" Jared said.

"I've never felt better in my life," he grinned, winking at Jared. He patted his bandaged arm. "Of course I'm still a little sore."

Amy sat in the middle of the couch. Michael sat down next to her, pulled the handsome little boy up on his lap.

"I'm glad we're all together," said Michael, clearing his throat. He looked over at his father nervously. "I've . . . we've got something to tell you. Amy and I are going to get married." His grin stretched clear across his face.

"But, I. . . ." Elijah began, looking from Michael to Jared, his eyebrows raised in question marks.

"Hey, that's fine!" Jared interrupted. "Congratulations to you both!"

"We'd like to get married while you're here, Jared," said Amy. "How long will you stay?"

"I had planned to leave this evening, but I guess I could stay on another day or two, if that wouldn't be rushing you."

Amy's voice tinkled musically with laughter.

"Not too soon. We want a simple ceremony," she said.

"Father," Michael said, "we would like to have you marry us, in your church, if you would."

"Why, yes," he muttered. He was confused by the sudden announcement. He had thought that by some miracle, Jared would marry Amy Robinson, but he never expected this. He looked over at Michael and Amy, saw them beaming at each other. He walked over and put his arm on Michael's shoulder. "I'm proud of you, son. Of course I'll marry you two. I insist upon it." He leaned over and pecked Amy on the cheek. "Welcome to the family. Come here, Joey. Sit on Grandpa's lap."

The old man's eyes glittered with a happiness he hadn't known for years.

"You've always been his grandfather," Michael said quietly. "I'm his real father."

Elijah was pleased at what Michael told him. He hid his surprise.

"Hey!" Bolt shouted, tossing his hat in the air. "I'm an uncle!" Confusion erupted as everyone exchanged embraces.

"Ten o'clock tomorrow morning," Michael announced. "Can you be ready by then, Amy?"

"I'm ready now," she smiled.

\* \* \* \* \* \* \* \* \* \*

Bolt was amazed to see the throng of people filing into the church when he rode up on his horse. Tom rode beside him. In front of him, his father and Michael rode in the family buggy.

Even though it was short notice, nearly everyone in the congregation had turned out for the wedding. It was only natural since the groom's father was the preacher and Amy's father was the choirmaster.

Storekeepers and merchants stood on their porches in front of falsefronts, watching the procession of gussied-up people who streamed by. Weddings brought out people's natural curiosity. A glimpse of the bride was what they wanted. An inspection of the groom.

A face caught Bolt's eye.

A second too late, the man across the street lowered the brim of his hat to hide his features. Will Atterbury.

On the outside, Bolt remained calm, jovial about his brother's wedding. But, inside his guts churned. His nerves jangled like snapped guitar strings. His heart beat like a grouse's wings.

When they reached the church, Bolt dismounted, handed his reins to Tom, who was still atop his horse.

"Take our horses out behind the church," he told Tom in a low voice. "Leave them close to the back door. Then come back around here. We'll go in the front way with the other guests. I'll wait for you."

Tom knew better than to question Bolt.

Bolt made himself visible while he waited for Tom. He stood at the entrance to the church, with his father, shaking hands and talking to neighbors he hadn't seen for five years.

When Tom got back, Bolt turned to his father.

"Do me a favor, will you, Father?" Bolt said. "Make this an extra long ceremony."

Jared and Tom entered the church. Once inside, Bolt headed for a little room in the back of the building where Michael was waiting nervously for the wedding to begin.

"Michael," said Jared. "You'll have to find someone else to stand up with you. Something came up. I got to leave."

"Now?"

"Now."

"Somebody after you?"

"Yeah. Sorry. Come on, Tom. This is one wedding we can't attend."

He darted out the back door, Tom Penrod on his heels.

## CHAPTER ELEVEN

After a week in the saddle, the 25c bath, including soap and towel, was pure luxury for the two men. The hot soaking relieved aching muscles, took the bite out of saddle-sore butts.

After their bath, Bolt and Penrod went to the barbershop on Dodge City's Front Street. A sign in the window proclaimed barber George Dieter as "the eminent tonsorial artist of the Arkansas Valley." Inside the Centennial Barber Shop, Bolt climbed into an adjustable chair, plunked his dusty boots on the footrest. Behind Dieter, tucked into individual cubbyholes, were rows of personalized shaving mugs, each inscribed with a customer's name and painted occupational symbol. The scents of hair tonic and powder hung in the air.

"Where can we get a good meal around here?" asked Bolt.

"You can't beat Beatty and Kelley's Restaurant for home cooking," said Dieter. "It's the first door west of here."

"If you want a steak," said Lemley, the barber who was shaving Tom, "go to Delmonico's Steak

House. They give you a mighty good hunk of meat for your money."

Dieter finished trimming Bolt's hair, handed him a small hand mirror.

"Do you know of any ranch property for sale?" Bolt asked as he handed the mirror back after checking the haircut.

"You can ask at the Land Office," said Dieter. "Or better yet, ask Bob Wright. He's kind of the top man here in Dodge. He knows everything that goes on. He can help ya."

"Where do I find this Wright?"

"He owns the General Store, right across from the railroad tracks."

"Thanks," said Bolt, climbing out of the chair. "How much do I owe you?"

"Ten cents for the shave. Two bits more for the haircut."

An hour later, the two hungry men were at Delmonico's, cutting into thick, juicy steaks. After eating beef jerky, hard tack and beans for a week, this, too, was a treat. After leaving the barbershop, Tom got their rooms at Dodge House while Bolt went to talk to Bob Wright at the general store. Wright was helpful, giving him leads on several large spreads that were for sale.

"This is what I call good food," Tom said.

"You'd think cow manure was good food," Bolt kidded.

"After your cooking. . . ."

"Whatdya mean, my cooking. The coffee you made tasted like horse piss." The two men were jovial, relaxed after the long ride. Being clean and having their bellies filled greatly improved their ragged dispositions. It was good to be in another town with new faces and nobody tracking them. They were sure they had lost the three men who were stalking them back in Abilene and Ellsworth.

"You know, Tom, that one ranch interests me. The Pike ranch. Wright said it had good water on it. That'll be an important factor if we're gonna raise cattle."

"What's this 'we' shit?" Tom grinned. "I'm just along for the ride."

"Hey, I thought we were partners."

"If the deal's clean and it don't cost me an arm and a leg."

"I don't know how clean it'll be. Wright said there were complications. Bernard Pike died a month ago. He left a son and a daughter and they want to sell out. Guess there's been some trouble about the water rights out there. We'll ride out in the morning, check the ranch out."

"Glad you said tomorrow. Because tonight I plan to tie one on at the Long Branch Saloon. Hey, Bolt, did you see them mugs at the barbers?"

"The ones on the shelves? Yeah, I saw 'em."

"Did ya see the pictures on them — the casket on the mortician's mug, a train on the railroad conductor's mug, the printing press on the printers...."

"Yeah, yeah, I saw 'em. What about them?"

Tom leaned back in his chair, tipped it on two legs, and laughed heartily.

"I was just wondering, Bolt. What kind of a picture they'd draw on a mug for you? You being the proud owner of a whorehouse." Tom's laughter drew stares from other diners.

"Well, I know what they'd put on your mug," Bolt retorted. "A horse's ass!"

"Speaking of ass and whorehouses, I'm going to go find me a woman. Want to join me?"

"Is that all you ever think about, Tom? Hell, no. I'm going to get a good night's sleep in a real bed. That hard ground gets tiresome in a hurry."

"Well, old man, see you later. Much later."

"Don't be too late. I want you to go with me out to the Pike spread in the morning."

\*\*\*\*\*\*\*\*\*\*

"Jared? Jared Bolt?"

The voice came from behind him as he walked through the lobby of the Dodge Hotel on his way to his room.

He turned around, stood eye-to-eye with a beautiful red-haired woman. The face looked familiar, but he couldn't place her.

"Don't you remember me, Jared? Sandra. Used to be Sandra Wissner. It's Sandra Jacobs now. We went to school together. Back in Ellsworth."

"Sandra? Yes, now I remember. I can't believe it. What are you doing in Dodge City?"

"We live here. My husband and I. We have a little farm here. Oh, I'm glad I came into the hotel tonight. I'm here visiting with my brother. He's the desk clerk."

"Well, it's nice to see you again after all these years. Let me look at you." He stepped back and took in her full beauty. Her blue eyes sparkled and her smile exposed white even teeth. She was tall and had a beautiful figure. Her brown dress seemed to accentuate her red hair. She reminded him of an oak tree, turning autumn. He didn't want to stare, but he couldn't help noticing her ample bosom that pushed against the material of her frock. "You're pretty, Sandra. If I remember right, you were always kind of . . . kind of pudgy." He wished he hadn't said it.

"Fat, you mean." She laughed. "And you, Jared, you've grown up to be quite a handsome man. You were always kind of ugly and scrawny."

"I reckon I deserved that."

"Jared, why don't you come over to my house? We can talk about old times. I live in the house behind the hotel. Just across the field. We can walk."

"I don't know. Your husband might not. . . ."

"My husband is gone right now. He's up at Fort Wallace. Been there for near a month. Won't be back for another month. Come on, Jared. I'll fix you something to eat."

"I just ate."

"Well, I'll fix you a drink, then. Come on." She latched her arm into his and pulled him toward the door.

Bolt didn't really want to go. He'd rather go right up to his room and go to sleep. Alone. But he felt it would be rude to refuse an old friend. They'd known each other since they were little children, had grown up together. Sandra's parents had lived close to his house.

"All right, Sandra. One drink for old times."

They walked the short distance from the Dodge Hotel to her house across a vacant field. The house was tucked in between two similar frame houses.

"Nice place you got here," said Bolt as they entered the livingroom.

"We like it. But it's lonesome with Virgil gone so much. I spend a lot of time with my brother and his family."

"What's your brother's name? I can't remember."

"Benny."

"That's right. He was a couple years older than we were."

"Still is. What would you like to drink?"

"You got some whiskey?"

"Yes. I'll get it."

Bolt watched her walk across the room, disappear into the kitchen. It was hard to realize that she was the same girl who used to be fat and . . . and yes, ugly. Little Sandra Wissner. She came back into the room, carrying a bottle and two glasses. She poured their two drinks and sat down on the couch next to Bolt.

"How's your father, Jared? Is he still preaching?"

"Yes. Getting the ills that come with old age."

"And your brother? Michael. Isn't that his name?"

"Yes. Michael just got married a week ago."

"He did? Who'd he marry? Anyone I know?"

"Amy Robinson." Bolt was sure that Sandra was aware of the scandal about him and Amy. She still lived in Ellsworth when he left home.

"Oh, yes. Amy. We moved from Ellsworth shortly after you left town. I wondered what happened to her. Did she . . . did she have a baby?"

"Yes. Michael's. A long story. How are your parents?"

"They're both gone. My father was a deputy and he was shot by an outlaw. My mother died a couple of months later. Of a broken heart, I think."

"I'm sorry to hear that."

"Yeah. But she lived long enough to see me married. She was happy for me." She was quiet for a few moments. The silence was awkward.

"Well, tell me about yourself, Jared. Are you married?"

"Nope. Never found the right girl. And they call me Bolt now. Just Bolt."

"Bolt it is." Her blue eyes locked into his. Her moist lips parted in a sensuous smile. She reached over and touched Bolt's hand.

"I meant what I said over at the hotel, Bolt. You are a very handsome man."

"And you are beautiful. I mean that."

"Bolt, I know you don't remember it, but do you know that you were the first boy to ever kiss me? When we were about seven or eight?"

"Yeah," he laughed. "I vaguely remember that. We thought we were so grown up."

"We're grown up now, Bolt." The look in her deep blue eyes said more than her words did. There was a sweet delicate hunger to them, a yearning. An unspoken invitation. Bolt recognized the passion that bubbled below the surface. A twinge of desire tugged at his loins.

Impulsively, she leaned over and kissed Bolt on the mouth. A delicate brush against his lips. Soft, sensual lips on his. Lips that lingered long enough to tell of lonesome days, empty nights. Fragile lips that parted passionately to accept his tongue.

Bolt slipped his arm around her thin waist, pulled her close to him. Firm pert breasts pressed against him. Her sweet scent, jasmine and delicate soap drifted to his nostrils. He ran his hands through the silken red hair that fell softly to her shoulders.

She backed away from the kiss, looked into Bolt's eyes.

"I want you," she said, a husk in her voice. "Is it so wrong to want you?"

"It's not wrong, Sandra."

"I've been so lonely. But, it's more than that, Bolt. There's something about you. A tenderness you have. The way you look at me. Your smile. I don't know what it is, but there's some magic about you that makes me feel all tingly inside."

"It's you, Sandra. You project a passion that few women possess. You're all woman."

"I guess women aren't supposed to have feelings of desire, but with you . . . well, I want you. Very much. Do you want me?"

He took her hand in his and placed it in his lap, rested it against the rigid bulge in his trousers.

"Yes. I want you very much." Bolt had not intended to get involved with Sandra, but the thing that was happening between them was natural. He firmly believed that the cruelest thing you could do to a woman was to turn her down when she wanted you. He also believed that whatever a man and woman did together was good as long as it wasn't forced and no one got hurt.

Without another word, Sandra stood up, took his hand and led him to her bedroom. She unbuttoned the tiny pearl buttons of her long-sleeved bodice, slipped it off her shoulders. She lifted the lace camisole over her head. Her firm rounded breasts jutted out proudly. She unfastened her long skirt and underskirt, let them drop to the floor. She stood facing Bolt, her dark thatch visible beneath sheer white panties.

Bolt undressed slowly, never taking his eyes off of her enticing creamy body. When he was naked, he came to her, held her in his arms, his swollen member rubbing against the smooth silkiness of her sheer panties.

He kissed her tenderly, passionately, his tongue darting into the sweetness of her mouth. She responded by pushing her tongue into his parted lips. Bolt felt her soft yielding body crush against him as she wriggled her thighs against his hardness.

Gently, he pushed her back onto the bed, pulled her panties down over her round buttocks, down past the nest of her sex, beyond her knees and ankles, until she lay there nude, inviting.

He got in bed next to her on the clean fragrant sheet. He placed a hand on her cheek, gazed into her pleading eyes and then kissed her again. He moved his hand down to a full firm breast, massaged it tenderly. She moaned with pleasure. He kissed her neck, nibbled his way down to her breast, found her nipple. He sucked the small kernal into his mouth, ran his tongue around its surface. It hardened with the friction. He squeezed her breast as he suckled, felt her body squirm against him.

When he slid his hand down her smooth body, across her flat tummy, to her furry mound, she shuddered with pleasure.

"That feels so good. Your touch," she gasped.

She reached down, grasped his manhood in her warm hand. Clutching the rigid organ, she slid her hand up and down its length, bringing the loose skin up around the mushroom head.

"Oh, you're so big. So big and good." She ran her forefinger across the slit tip, felt the slippery substance that leaked out. Delicately, she smeared the clear fluid around the sensitive head.

Bolt thrust his thighs upward, fully aroused by her loving stimulation. He liked the way she stroked his erection, the way she slid her cupped hand down to the base of his stalk, then brought it up over the sensitive head.

He let his hand glide across the bare flesh of her inner thighs, brush against the soft furred mound of her sex. She responded to his touch, squirming with passion.

Bolt was ready. He wanted to be inside her honey pot.

"Do you want me inside?" he husked.

She paused for a moment.

"Bolt. I want to do something. I want to kiss this." She squeezed his manhood to show him what she meant. "I want to put it in my mouth. I want to know what it feels like to have it in my mouth. Do you think I'm bad for wanting to try it?"

No, he didn't think she was bad.

Sandra was good.

Damned good.

## CHAPTER TWELVE

The twitch was involuntary.
It came when she spoke the words. A tug at his manhood when he thought about what she wanted to do.
"I think it would be right fine," Bolt husked.
"I've never done it before, but I've wanted to. I've wondered what it would feel like. I've been afraid to do it because I thought it was bad."
"Nothing's bad if it's natural and makes you happy. Do it to me, Sandra."
She lowered her head to his loins, still clutching his shaft in her hand. She touched her lips to the tip of his cock, brushing it with a fleeting kiss. Tingling shocks coursed through his loins. Her moist lips parted as she took the sensitive mushroom head into her mouth. She circled her tongue around the smooth surface, tasted the lemony fluid. She took his cock deeper into her mouth, sucking it with sensuous lips, covering it with her warm dampness. She felt it throb with little spasms of pleasure. She bobbed up and down on his rigid organ, sucked on it until her cheeks hollowed.

He reached up, put his hand on her silken hair, pulled her head down on him. He thrust his organ deeper into her warm mouth. He was on the delicate edge, ready to spill his seed at the slightest movement. He held her head still, staying his explosion.

"Let me inside you. Before it's too late."

She rolled over on her back, spreading her legs. He came to her, his hot spear wavering above her sex cleft. He lowered himself, pressed against her damp entrance with his spearhead. Slowly, he entered her oiled passageway, the lips parting with the gentle nudge of his shaft. He slid in easily, pushed into the core of her sex. His swollen organ rubbed against her hidden love button, exerting a pressure that excited her. He felt her shudder beneath him as orgasm rocked her frame.

He stroked her, slowly at first. He felt the muscles of her sheath tighten around his pulsating organ. Her undulating body rippled beneath him. He dipped deep into her honeypot, savoring the sweetness.

It felt good to be with a warm responsive woman. A woman who was comfortable with her sexuality, who wasn't afraid to experiment and grow from that experience. He had been with women who were pushy and aggressive. Like the first girl he'd had, Amy Robinson. He'd been with women who wanted to be loved but were unresponsive when they got to the bed. Yet they were all different. All mysterious. All had something to give. Something to take.

He plunged his shaft deep inside the warm tight sheath. His rhythm was slow, deliberate, at first.

He felt her thrust her pussy up to meet him. She was soft and yielding beneath him. His strokes became faster, deeper, as he penetrated to her boiling depths. Finally, he knew he could no longer hold back. He grabbed her smooth, bare shoulder, squeezed it gently as his milky seed bubbled up and exploded against the walls of her steaming cauldron.

Later, when Bolt was dressing, Sandra looked over at him, full of a contentment she had not known before.

"Bolt, you're a good man. You showed me something tonight. I feel so alive, so complete."

He smiled at her.

"You *are* alive, Sandra. You're a very loving woman. A good person. Don't ever forget it."

"Bolt," she said as he was leaving, "I hope you'll come back some time. But, if you don't, I'll think about you."

"Thank you, lovely lady."

And then he was gone.

\* \* \* \* \* \* \* \* \* \*

The blood curdling scream pierced the brisk morning air.

There was only one scream.

And then it was quiet.

Dead quiet.

A woman's scream, Bolt was sure.

He was on his way to the Pike ranch to check it out, about a quarter a mile further on. Tom was still asleep when he left. Too much carousing the night before.

Bolt spurred his horse to a gallop.

Five minutes later, he rode up to the house, dismounted. He looped the reins over the hitchrail. His eyes quickly scanned the area, searching for some clue to the cause of the woman's scream. He saw nothing unusual. He ran up to the house, knocked loudly on the door. He heard no sound from inside.

A dog barked from somewhere out back. Bolt ran around the house. There were several outbuildings: a stable, a barn, a chicken coop, storage shed. He ran to the barn, looked inside. Nothing. The mongrel dog came up to him, yipped at him, followed him while he checked the other buildings.

He saw the woman's body first. Inside the slatted fence that served as a chicken yard, near the wooden chicken coop. At first glance, the form looked like a pile of discarded rags. He unlatched the gate, swung it open, and ran over to the still figure.

"Lady, you all right?" he asked, shaking her shoulder.

She opened her eyes, started to sit up. When she saw Bolt, she fainted.

That's when Bolt saw it. A man's hand lying in the dirt, chopped off at the wrist. Chickens were pecking at the bloody stump. Bolt fought back the bile that rose from his stomach. Another detached hand, over by the chicken coop was being clucked over by a rooster.

Bolt dashed over to the chicken coop, looked inside.

A young man lay sprawled on the ground, his throat slit from ear to ear. Blood stained the earth beneath the body. Vacant eyes stared up at the ceiling. The man's mouth hung open, frozen in a grotesque, crooked grin. His arms, folded neatly across his chest, ended in bloody stumps where the hands had been.

Bolt dashed back out, sick in his guts. He looked down at the unconscious girl. Her long dark hair stuck out of a red bandanna. Dirt and chicken droppings clung to it. A basket lay beside her.

He leaned down, patted her cheeks. Her eyelids fluttered open. When she saw Bolt, her brown eyes widened in terror. She tried to scoot away from him.

"It's all right, Miss. I'm a friend. I want to help you." He slipped his arm under hers, helped her to her feet.

"Who . . . who are you?" she asked, her voice trembling.

"The name is Bolt. Come on. I'll help you into the house." He didn't know what had happened, but he didn't want her to look at the grisly sight again. He knew she had already seen it.

He steadied her as she walked on rubbery legs, her slim body pressed against his. They went in the back door, into the kitchen, where she eased into a wooden chair.

"There . . . there's coffee made . . . if you'd . . . like to pour some." Her soft voice quivered. Her brown eyes were fixed in a blank stare. Bolt knew she was in shock.

"What's your name?" Bolt asked softly after he had poured two cups of steaming coffee, set one on the table in front of her. He pulled a chair out from the table, sat across from her.

"A . . . Anita. Anita P-p-pike." She cupped her hands around the mug, as if to warm them.

"Anita, who was that out . . . out there?"

She looked down, stared into the coffee cup.

"My brother," she said, her voice barely audible. Her tone was flat, emotionless. "My brother, Paul. That was Paul out there in the. . . ."

And then it hit her full force. She jumped up out of the chair, flung her arms in the air, spilling coffee down the front of her dress. She screamed, the same ear-piercing scream Bolt had heard earlier. She screamed again and again, hysterical.

"Paul's dead! My brother's dead! Murdered! Paul was murdered!" She began to weep, her body heaving with deep sobs.

Bolt grabbed her by the shoulders, drew her close.

"Go ahead and cry Anita. Let it all out."

Her small form convulsed with grief. He held her close until her trembling subsided.

She looked up at him with red-rimmed eyes. Tears streaked her smooth cheeks.

"I'm all right now," she said.

He released her and stepped back.

"I'm sorry, Anita. About your brother."

"Yes. It's so sad. He is . . . was such a good person. I'm glad Pap didn't live to see this. Papa died a month ago. And now Paul."

"Do you have any idea who . . . who killed your brother?"

"Yes. It had to be the Guthrie brothers. They've been trouble ever since they moved in.

Oh, I can't believe Paul's dead. I went out to gather the eggs this morning and when I went in the chicken coop . . . he was just . . . just lying there . . . dead. I was standing in the doorway and I turned around to see if I could see anyone. I didn't see nobody around. Didn't hear anything. That's when I saw his . . . hands, and those chickens. . . ." She paused, took a deep breath and then continued. "Paul and I ate breakfast early and then he went out to do the chores. I didn't go out to gather the eggs until about an hour later 'cause I was busy. I wanted to get the dishes done up and make the beds. Paul was such a good boy. Everybody liked him."

"I'm sure they did," Bolt said. But he knew different. Someone must have hated Paul very much to murder him that way. Paul's death had been very brutal, vengeful. The way his throat had been slashed. Then the cruelty of chopping off his hands and tossing them out for chicken feed.

"You said your father died a month ago. How did he die, Anita?"

"It was an accident. He got throwed from his horse. At least that's how the sheriff figured it happened. Papa went out to repair the fence. His horse stumbled in a ditch and Papa fell off. Cracked his head against a big rock. When Papa's horse came back home that day without Papa, Paul knew something was wrong. He went out lookin' for Papa and came across him out in the field. The back of his head was all bloody and bashed in."

"And his horse. It wasn't hurt?" Seemed odd to Bolt that a horse could take a spill hard enough to kill a man and not break a leg.

"No. The horse just came back home without Papa. Paul thought there was something suspicious about Papa's death. He said he thought the Guthrie boys had somethin' to do with it. That's why he went to the sheriff. The sheriff came out and investigated, but he said it was accidental."

"Tell me about the Guthrie brothers. Bob Wright, at the general store, told me there had been some trouble over the water rights. Was it the Guthrie boys?"

"Yes. There was a lot of trouble when Papa was still alive. They wanted our water. They bought the property next to ours to raise cattle. But it's bad land. No grazing land and no water on it. First they tried to claim that the big watering hole on our north forty belonged to them. But Papa proved it was on our property. We got the rights to that water, all clear and legal. Then one day Papa caught Clay — that's the youngest brother — cutting the fence again, so's their cattle could use our watering place. Papa warned him to get out and stay off our land. Clay got mad and shot at Papa. He hit him in the leg. Papa shot back and hit Clay in the hand. Clay got on his horse and rode back home, but he yelled at Papa. Said he would get even with him. That's why Paul and I thought those boys killed Papa."

"And you think they killed Paul?"

"Yes. I'm sure of it. After Papa died, Paul and I decided to sell the ranch. The Guthrie brothers came over a week after Papa died. They was actin' real sorry about Papa's death, saying what a terrible accident it was. They wanted to buy our ranch, but Paul told them he'd never sell to them. He got the shotgun and chased them off, told them not to ever come back. Wes, the older one, told Paul that they'd get our land, one way or another. I just know they killed Paul."

"Wright told me you were planning to sell. That's why I'm here. I'm looking for a nice ranch where I can settle down."

"We almost sold the ranch last week. To a Texan who had a lot of money. He was willing to pay us a fair price. But then Jake said we'd be foolish to sell. He wanted us to keep the ranch."

Bolt's eyebrows shot up.

"Who's Jake?"

"Jake Brady. He's the man I'm engaged to. He said we should keep the ranch and he'd help us with the work. But Paul didn't like that idea. He didn't take to Jake much, but that's 'cause he didn't know him like I do."

"How long you been engaged, Anita?"

"A week. We just got engaged a week ago. Jake'll be real upset about Paul, I know. He liked Paul, even though Paul was rude to him. Just last night Paul told Jake to get out of here and leave me alone. I don't know why Paul didn't like him. He's real nice and he's been tryin' to help us."

"How long have you known Jake?"

"He came by a few days after Papa died. Said he was new in town and that he'd heard about Papa. Said he was needin' work and wondered if we needed help. He's been over here a lot and we fell in love. We told Paul last night that we were fixin' to get married next week. Couldn't see any sense in waiting any longer. That's when Paul got mad and ordered him off the place.

"Anita, have you got a blanket I could use? I want to cover Paul's body until we can bury him."

"Yes, just a minute." She went to Paul's bedroom, removed a blanket from his bed and handed it to Bolt.

Bolt went back out to the chicken coop. He picked up the two bloody hands and carried them inside the small building, placed them beside the body. Loose dirt on the ground showed evidence of the struggle that had taken place. With a shudder, Bolt wondered if Paul was still alive when his hands were chopped from his body.

He almost missed it.

It was the same color as the earth.

He stooped over and picked it up.

A small swatch of cloth. About the size of his thumb. He turned it over in his hand, studied it. A piece of shirt or pants? No. It had only one ragged edge. The other three were smooth, finished. If it had been torn from a shirt, it would be ragged on all sides. A ribbon. That's what it looked like. The end of a ribbon. Only it was too thick for that.

He scrutinized the clothing Paul was wearing. One thing for sure. It hadn't come from anything Paul was wearing.

He tucked the small piece of cloth into his shirt pocket. He would ask Anita about it later.

"I'm going in to town to get the sheriff, Anita." he said when he went back in the house. "Will you be all right?"

"Yes. I'm all right."

Bolt mounted his horse, headed in the opposite direction. He had no intention of going to the sheriff just yet. He was going to call on the Guthrie brothers.

## CHAPTER THIRTEEN

Bolt didn't make it all the way to the Guthrie ranch.

They were waiting for him in the bushes.

"Hold it right there, Mister," said Wes Guthrie as he stepped out from behind a bush.

Bolt went for his pistol. Before he could draw it, the other two men stepped out. He was braced. Three .45 snouts pointed at his head.

"Take your pistol out nice and easy," demanded Eddie. "Drop it to the ground."

Bolt hesitated a moment. They had him cold. He eased his Colt out of its sheath, let it fall to the ground.

"Now get down off your horse," said Clay. Bolt looked at the man, saw the withered hand that hung limp and useless from his arm.

"You must be the Guthrie brothers," Bolt said. "I've heard about you." He swung his leg over his horse, lowered himself and let go of the saddle horn.

"What were you doing nosin' around the Pike ranch?" asked Wes. "We been watching the place. Saw your horse there and saw you walkin' around."

"Makes no difference why I was there. You killed Paul, didn't you?"

He heard the hammer of Eddie's pistol click.

"Not yet," Wes warned Eddie. He turned to Bolt.

"What's your name, cowboy?"

"None of your business."

Wes walked towards Bolt. He was a tall, thin man. A scar streaked down one side of his face.

"That's a funny name. Now cough it up, Mister!"

"Bolt. Just Bolt."

"That's good enough, Bolt. Now what's your connection with the Pike's? Start talkin', Mister."

"No connection," said Bolt. "Just interested in buying the place, that's all."

"You ain't buyin' nothing," said Wes. He paced to a spot directly in front of Bolt. He poked the pistol barrel at Bolt's stomach.

"Yeah," said Clay. "That land belongs to us. Soon's Jake and Anita are married."

"Shut up, Clay!" ordered Wes. He turned his head.

Just long enough for Bolt to react.

"You filthy scum!" yelled Bolt as he brought his left arm up, knocking the pistol from Wes' hand. With lightning speed, Bolt's right fist plowed into Wes' scarred face.

Wes struck back, catching Bolt in the stomach. Both men landed on the ground, wrestled for advantage.

Eddie lined up a shot, started to squeeze the trigger. Wes rolled Bolt over, was on top of him.

Eddie held his fire.

Bolt's pistol lay on the ground, two feet away. He whipped his hand upward, caught Wes across the throat. Wes grunted as the sharp edge of the hand brushed his Adam's apple.

Bolt shoved the heavy man off of him, reached for his gun with his left hand.

A boot crashed down on his arm.

Clay's boot.

Bolt grabbed Clay's leg with his good arm, toppled him to the ground. Bolt scooted sideways, ducked as Wes came after him. Wes tripped over his brother, crashed to the ground with a thud.

Bolt used his advantage. He smashed Wes in the jaw. Blood spurted from the mouth of the scar-faced man. Bolt struck him again, puffing his eye.

Eddie moved in close, tried to nail Bolt. But Bolt was quick. He was everywhere. He was nowhere.

Clay started to get up.

Bolt jumped to his feet, kicked Clay in the side of the head. Then he brought his boot heel down in the middle of Clay's stomach. Once. Twice. A third time.

Eddie moved in on Bolt.

Wes regained his stance. Plunged at Bolt.

The butt of Eddie's pistol crashed into the back of Bolt's head.

Everything went black.

Bolt sank into the darkness.

\* \* \* \* \* \* \* \* \* \*

"Oh, Jake, I'm so glad you're here." Anita ran her hands over her cheeks, wiping away the tears.

"What's the matter, Anita? You've been crying."

"It's Paul. He's been . . . murdered! The Guthrie boys did it. I'm sure."

"Anita, I can't believe that."

"It's true. Out in the chicken coop. Oh, it was terrible. I fainted and a man named Bolt found me out there. He's gone for the sheriff now. Jake, I just don't know what I'm going to do."

"Don't worry about it now. I'll take care of you."

He put his arms around her slim waist, drew her close to him. He took her inside the house, into the livingroom, where he held her for a long time, stroking her long silken hair.

"What was that man Bolt doing here?"

"He heard this place was for sale. He just came out to look at it. Said he was interested in buying it."

"Well, it's not for sale!" Jake's reply was a little too quick, too firm.

It surprised her.

"Jake, I know you wanted to keep the ranch and live here after we're married. But, I don't know. Now that . . . now that Paul's dead . . . I just don't think I want to live here. Not after seeing Paul that way. It would haunt me. I think I'd rather sell out to Bolt and move far away. You wouldn't mind, would you, Jake?"

"Let's not talk about it now, Anita. You're too upset."

"But I've got enough money so that we could move somewhere else. Start a new life. Papa left a lot of money and it . . . it's all mine now. Now that Paul is gone."

"But you've got good cattle land. The best around these parts. It would take a lot of money to settle somewhere else."

"I've got enough. There's over fifty thousand in the bank. We'll never have to worry about anything. Please, Jake."

She didn't detect the look on Jake's face.

Anita sat down on the couch, then got up a moment later. She picked up a small vase from a table, stroked it, set it down again. It was as if she didn't know what to do with her hands. Images of her brother flashed in her mind. His disembodied hands. The chickens pecking at them. She struggled to keep her sanity. She wanted to scream. She wanted to wake up and find out it was all just a bad dream.

It was no use. Finally, she turned to Jake.

"I need some more coffee. Would you like some?"

"Sure."

She turned and walked out of the room.

Jake did some quick figuring in his head. Fifty thousand on top of whatever they could get for the ranch. That sure as hell beat the thousand the Guthrie brothers offered him for his part in this little hoax. Wes had already paid him five hundred. Said he'd pay the other five after he and Anita were married. When Anita signed over the land deed to him and he signed it over to the Guthrie boys. Then he was supposed to do a disappearing act.

He had thought it was an easy way to pick up an extra thousand. But, he hadn't counted on the murder when he agreed to the deal.

It was necessary, he knew. Paul was causing too much of a ruckus about the wedding. The Guthrie boys said that Paul had to be out of the picture anyway. Otherwise Anita couldn't sign over the papers without Paul's approval. Wes had told him he'd make it worth his while if he helped get rid of Paul. He'd hinted at an extra thousand dollars.

Chicken feed compared to what he could get on his own. If he worked it right, he could marry Anita, take her for every penny she had, then split town in a hurry. Cut the Guthrie brothers out completely.

He wished he hadn't been involved in Paul's death. He wished he hadn't been the one to slit his throat. That was the hold the Guthrie brothers had over him.

Damn, that had been ugly. Clay was supposed to be standing watch with Eddie. But he came in with an axe and started chopping Paul's hands off, laughing all the time he was doing it. Crazy. Said he wanted revenge for what Paul's Pa had done to his hand. Clay was plumb out of his mind. Those hands. That's what made it gruesome.

Hell, let the Guthrie boys take the blame for it. Anita thinks they did it. And they did, really. They wouldn't like the doublecross he was planning, but they'd be strung up by the neck. He and Anita would see to that before they found him.

"Here, Jake," Anita said, placing a cup on a table near Jake's chair.

"Anita, let's get married right away. Go ahead and sell the ranch to Bolt. I realize it would be too upsetting for you to stay on here. We'll find another place."

She smiled up at him, pleased that he had changed his mind.

"Thank you, Jake. I knew you'd understand."

"You're mighty pretty, Anita," he grinned.

And he knew, then, that his plan would work.

## CHAPTER FOURTEEN

Bolt drifted in and out of consciousness. Fragments of voices floated in the air, then faded.

Loud, sharp words.

The confusion of one voice on top of another until they all blended together to form a ringing maze.

Then, the hum of silence.

In his stupor, he tried to separate the voices. He struggled to snatch a word from the muddy murmur, remember it, identify it. But each word dissipated before he could grasp it.

His eyes fluttered open. Everything blurred together in a guazy haze. Shadowy figures hovered above him. The forms seemed to revolve mysteriously, like a kalaidoscope until all shape and color melted into a gray nothingness.

When the threads of awareness penetrated his brain again, he fought to stay alert. He strained to distill the truth from the bombardment of confusion. He tried to raise his head, but was driven back by a stabbing pain that seared his skull.

The voices again.

Layers of voices.

"He's still alive."

"Let's finish him off."

"No."

"Now."

"Not now."

"Torture him."

"Make him suffer."

*Kill! Suffer! Humiliate! Torture!*

Bolt tried to scream but he was voiceless.

"Eddie, bring our horses over here," ordered Wes Guthrie. "Clay, go help him."

Five minutes later, the two brothers returned, leading the horses that had been stashed.

"You'll be a sorry sonofabitch when we get through with you, Mister Bolt," said Wes, jamming a boot into Bolt's ribs. "Nobody lays a hand on a Guthrie unless he pays the price. Hand me a rope, Clay."

Clay reached up, removed a rope from his saddle horn.

"Yeah, Wes, tie him up real good. Leave him for the vultures!" Clay tipped his head back and laughed insanely.

"I say kill him now. Fill him up with lead." Eddie waved his pistol at the man sprawled on the ground.

"Eddie, you're trigger happy," said Wes. "No, I've got something better planned for this nosy bastard."

He stooped down, drew Bolt's ankles together, then looped the rope around them. He wound the rope around the ankles three times, snugged them together, made a knot and tested it. He took the other end of the long rope and secured it to the saddle horn of Bolt's horse. With a smaller rope, he tied Bolt's wrists together, fastened them at Bolt's waist by winding the rope around his body. With a stiff hand, he slapped Bolt hard across the face, then backhanded him.

"Wake up, Bolt. This is one trip I want you to enjoy!"

Bolt forced his eyes open, tried to focus on his surroundings. He was barely conscious, but fear nagged at his brain, prickled his nerves. He felt the restraint of the tight ropes around his ankles and wrists. Through filmy eyes, he saw the rump of the horse above him. The length of rope that crossed the rump. He felt a gentle tug at his legs as his horse moved slightly, restless in its place.

Panic gripped him as his hazy mind realized what was happening. He tried to free his hands, but it was useless.

Wes held the reins of Bolt's horse in his hand as he mounted his own horse. Wes wrapped the reins of Bolt's horse around his hand. Clenched his fist. With one swift kick to his flanks, Wes' horse took off. He pulled Bolt's horse behind him.

Clay and Eddie followed on their horses.

Bolt's body slid along the earth, slow and easy at first. As the horses picked up speed, his limp body began to bounce in the dirt. Small rocks ripped at the back of his shirt, scraped the bare flesh. The back of his head, which was already bruised, struck a small rock, shooting pain through his skull. His buttocks bumped along, smashing into the hard earth.

He struggled to remain conscious. Blood oozed from the raw wounds on his back and head, leaving a mottled spoor on the earth behind him.

He tried again to free his hands. He kicked at the rope holding his feet in mid-air. Using every muscle and every bit of strength he could summon, he flipped himself over on his left side.

Twigs and small pebbles gouged at his side, ripping the flesh. The rough earth shredded his cheek. A rock jabbed at the bone under his eye. The uneven ground tossed him onto his back again. Dirt and small rocks ate at his trousers until particles of blood-stained cloth clung to the earth.

When he could no longer stand the pain, he flopped his head to the other side. His cheek bone pounded against the ground. His neck twisted grotesquely, jarred by every slap at the dirt. Chunks of hair ripped from his skull, stuck to leaves and twigs and rocks. Pebbles tore at his skin. A sharp rock poked a hole on the side of his forehead.

The faster the horses went, the higher in the air he bounced. The harder he smashed to the ground. Raw flesh pounded against the rough earth. Bones crashed into the hard dirt. Muscles twisted and stretched and tore. Pain pounded on top of pain. Fire burned at the gaping wounds.

Somewhere in the back of his mind, Bolt remembered something his father used to preach. *God shall not let you suffer more pain than you can bear.* He questioned the truth of that statement. He had reached the point where he didn't think he could stand any more pain. He felt like everything inside and out was broken. Shattered.

Splintered. He knew he was going to die. He waited for the final crushing blow.

It didn't come.

Only more brutal pounding against the unyielding earth. *Ashes to ashes, dust to dust.* He knew the end was near.

Voices intruded on his confused mind.

"Faster! Go faster, Wes!"

"Cut him loose! Leave him for the buzzards!"

Insane laughter mingled with the shouts.

He prayed for oblivion. The battering of his broken body continued as he slapped over and over against the hard earth.

Each jolt shot a color of pain to his brain. A stab of red. A jab of blue. Green and yellow hammered to the core. His brain swirled with the whirlpool of pure agony where the colors fused together, turned gray.

Finally, his mind was sucked into a deep whirling black hole.

Mercifully, he slipped into unconsciousness.

\* \* \* \* \* \* \* \* \* \*

His mind racing with the new scheme, Jake Brady left the Pike ranch. It would be tricky, but he could pull it off.

His instinct was to head for the sheriff's office, catch up with Bolt. He wanted to talk to him, make sure that Bolt would buy the Pike ranch. Somehow, he had to get his hands on Bolt's money.

But that would have to wait till later. First, he had to report in to the Guthrie brothers. It wouldn't do to arouse their suspicions now. He had to play along with them a little while longer. At least until he was in a position to get all of Anita's money.

He would check in with the Guthries as Wes had ordered. He would tell them that he had seen Anita, that plans were being made for an immediate marriage. He would assure them that Anita would put the ranch in his name and that he, in turn, would sign the deed over to them. He didn't want them to know about the money she had in the bank.

When he arrived at the Guthrie ranch, he saw the three brothers out in the front yard. They were hovering over something on the ground. A dead animal? That's what it looked like at first. A dead calf or small horse. Fresh blood stained the earth. Jake came closer, hopped down from his horse. And then he saw what it was.

A man.

A bloody, bruised human being.

"Who's that?" asked Jake, repulsed by the sight of the battered body that was still attached to the horse by a long rope.

"Says his name's Bolt," replied Wes.

"Said he was going to buy the Pike ranch," added Clay.

"Yeah," said Eddie, "that would spoil our plans."

"Is he dead?" asked Jake.

"He's still breathing," said Wes, "but that's about all." He untied the rope from Bolt's saddle horn, let it drop to the ground.

"Let's finish him off," said Eddie.

"He's already buzzard bait," said Wes. "Leave him be."

"Yeah," cackled Clay, "let the sun bake his brain!"

Wes ignored his crazy brother and turned to Jake. "How'd it go with Anita?"

"Well," said Jake, "she's a mite upset. But I think she's willing to get married right away. She needs me now that she's alone."

Jake had to stall. He needed more time to think. Damn, he needed this man who was dying on the ground. Alive, Bolt was worth about eight or ten thousand dollars to him, he figured. Dead, he wasn't worth a damn."

"I want action," said Wes. "We don't have time to wait while you and Anita pussy foot around. Be sure to get that land deed signed over to us right away. After we get that, you'll get your other five hundred."

"I've got an idea," Jake said. "Would clear us in Paul's death. I'll deliver Bolt to the sheriff. Hang Paul's death on him. Tell the sheriff we saw him killing Pike and that we dragged him off. After all, he was at the Pike ranch. And he's a new man in town. It'll simplify things. Keep us in the clear."

"Don't know," said Wes. "Sounds complicated to me."

"Well, Anita is positive you boys killed her brother. She also thinks you're responsible for her father's death. If she gets to the sheriff, you boys will have the law down on you. And the townspeople. Maybe a lynch mob. Now, if we come up with the killer first . . . well, the sheriff will believe us."

"You got a point," said Wes. Resentment began to boil up in Wes' guts. Jake's words had come across as a threat, insinuating that Anita could nail them if Jake wanted her to. Hell, Wes could prove that Jake killed Paul, if necessary. But that would mess things up. He needed Jake to get that Pike land, and Jake knew it. The sonofabitch. Things were going too easy for Jake, Wes thought. He didn't trust Jake, but he did have a point. Let Bolt take the rap for Paul's death.

"I think you may be right," said Wes. "Take Bolt to the sheriff. Tell him your story. You'd better be convincing. Won't matter much whether Bolt's dead or alive when you get there. Just keep the Guthrie name out of it!"

"It'll work. Just let me handle it. Then I'll take care of the other things. Have you got a buckboard I can use to take him in?"

"Yeah. Out by the stables. Eddie, Clay, get it. Hook it up to Bolt's horse. Help Jake load this bastard."

He kicked Bolt in the shoulder.

Clay and Eddie quickly brought the buckboard, hooked Bolt's horse and Jake's horse to it.

"Get my rope off him," ordered Wes.

Eddie untied Bolt's ankles while Clay fumbled with the knot at his wrists. When the rope was free, Eddie picked up Bolt's legs. Clay grabbed him under the arms. They started to swing him up on the buckboard. Jake stepped up and supported Bolt's back, easing the jolt of the dead weight hitting the floor of the wagon.

As he rode away, Jake thought about the man in the buckboard. God, he hoped the man lived. He wanted all the money he could get on this deal.

He didn't know what to do with Bolt for now. He sure as hell wasn't going to deliver him to the law. He should take him to the doctor, but there might be too many questions. Maybe he'd take him to Anita's. Hide him out there until he could get his money.

Jake pulled the buckboard around to the back of Anita's house. He heard the man groan before he climbed down from the seat of the buckboard. He walked around to the side of the open wagon, saw Bolt's eyes flutter open. Anita was heading in his direction, walking across the open field behind the house.

"I just buried Paul," she said somberly. "Next to Papa."

Perspiration trickled down her face, drenched her clothing. A smudge of dirt was on her cheek. She raised her arm, wiped a sleeve across her damp face.

"You should have waited, Anita. I'd have done it for you!"

"It was something I had to do myself, Jake. But thanks."

And then she saw Bolt's bloody body in the buckboard. She gasped.

"My God, what happened?"

"Rough, isn't it? The Guthrie boys. They did it. Same as they killed Paul. Only, Bolt's still alive. I saved his life. They were torturing him. Planned to kill him. But I stopped them."

"Oh, Jake, you're so brave. I knew the Guthrie brothers killed Paul." She placed a hand on Bolt's feverish forehead. He opened his eyes, looked up at her. Her cool hand on his brow felt soothing to him.

"Bolt, are you all right?" Her soft voice tinkled like faint music. With difficulty, he opened his parched lips.

"Ye . . . eeesss."

"Jake, we've got to get him inside and take care of him."

"Maybe I should take him in to the doctor."

"No. He'd never make it. Help me, will you?"

Together, they carefully scooted Bolt to the back edge of the buckboard. Jake slipped his arm under Bolt's arm, pulled him gently to a sitting position, lifted his legs over the side.

Bolt grimaced with pain.

"Can you make it, Bolt?" Anita asked tenderly. "We'll take care of you."

Pain stabbed at the back of Bolt's head as he nodded. He let himself down gently until he was between Jake and Anita. He put one arm around each of them, his weight on their shoulders. They half-carried, half-dragged him inside the house.

"Put him on Papa's bed."

They struggled with Bolt's weight until they got him into the bedroom. Anita reached down and flipped the covers back, then helped Jake lower the wounded man to the bed.

Bolt sat on the side of the bed, his feet dangling.

"Water," Bolt husked. His mouth and throat were dry as parched corn husks. His teeth crunched down on dirt and grit. His eyes were puffed to slits.

Anita disappeared and returned a moment later with a glass of water. She held it to his lips, tilted it while he sipped from it.

Bolt's face contorted in pain as he lay down on the bed, aided by Anita's delicate touch and Jake's strength. He looked up at the girl hovering over him. Anita looked so small, so frail. She blew a wisp of hair away from her eyes, felt Bolt's forehead again. He didn't want her to move her soft hand. It felt so good.

Bolt blinked his eyes and looked at the man who had rescued him from the Guthrie brothers. The man Anita was going to marry. Jake seemed too big for Anita, somehow. He was tall and gangly, big-boned, clumsy-looking. There was something about Jake that Bolt didn't like. Hell, he should be grateful to the man for saving his life. And he was grateful. But, something about Jake grated on his nerves. Maybe it was his eyes. Jake's dark brown eyes projected something evil, something devious.

And Jake's hat. That bothered him, too. Bolt thought he was going crazy. Why would another man's hat bother him? Maybe it was the fact that Jake wore the hat inside the house. Damn, if that wasn't crazy thinking. Jake had been too busy helping him get in bed to remove his hat.

Finally, Bolt closed his eyes. He could no longer think about hats or Jake, or Anita, or anything else. He was sapped of all energy.

"Let him sleep a while," said Anita. "I'll clean him up later."

"Anita, can we talk?" asked Jake.

"Sure. Let's go in the livingroom." Anita noticed that Jake was nervous, fidgity. It bothered her for a moment until she thought about all the violence that had happened that day. It was enough to make any man jumpy.

"Anita," Jake said when they settled on the couch. "Let's get married tomorrow morning. Then we can take the afternoon stage to Cheyenne the day after, on Friday. I've got a lot of money in the Cheyenne bank," he lied. "We can draw your money out of the bank here, then go to Cheyenne, get my money and then we can go wherever we want to."

"That's too soon, Jake," she protested. "I need to buy a wedding dress and I'd have to sell the ranch first."

"You don't need a wedding dress. We can buy you all the clothes you want in Cheyenne. You've got no family now. No need to have a fancy wedding. Or if you'd rather, we could wait and get married in Cheyenne. You said Bolt wanted to buy your ranch. I'm sure that by Friday he'll be well enough so that you can sign over the deed to him and get the money. I can help you with that."

Jake hoped he was right about Bolt. Otherwise, he'd have to settle for the money Anita had in the bank.

"I want to get married in this house, Jake. I guess you're right about not having a fancy wedding. But I do want a new dress. We have to arrange for the preacher to come out here. And, we could sell the ranch later if Bolt doesn't buy it. Tomorrow's too soon. This is Wednesday. We could get married Friday morning and still make the afternoon stage that day."

"That's my girl." He put his arm around her, hugged her. "Friday it is."

"What time?"

"About eleven, I'd say. Give us time to have lunch before the stage comes."

"I've got a lot to do. Hope I can get it all done by Friday."

Jake smiled. "You will. I'll have the preacher out here at eleven, Friday morning."

Bolt's eyes were closed in the other room. But he wasn't asleep. He heard every word of the conversation between Jake and Anita. He didn't like what he heard. He knew that Jake was marrying Anita for her money. Probably his own, too, if he bought the ranch.

# CHAPTER FIFTEEN

His head was full of wet cobwebs.

It took him a moment to realize where he was. He had slept all afternoon. When he tried to sit up, the pain that stabbed through his head drove him back down. He ached in every muscle in his body.

A moment later, Anita was at his bedside.

"How are you feeling?" she asked softly.

"Like a dog trampled by stampeding cattle."

"That good, huh?"

They both smiled.

Slowly, methodically, Bolt pulled himself to a sitting position. Anita began unbuttoning Bolt's dirty, blood-stained shirt. The back of the shirt was mostly torn away. Shreds of cloth stuck to open wounds, fastened there by dried blood. Bolt winced as she tried to remove the shirt.

"I'll get some warm water and soak it off. Then I'll clean your wounds." She picked up a white porcelain bowl off the floor and set it on the table next to the bed. "Here's the chamber pot if you need to use it."

She left the bedroom to get the things she needed.

Bolt looked down at his dirty, dusty clothes. Blood stains spattered the Levi's, the torn blue flannel shirt. He brushed at his chest, knocking away the loose dirt.

That's when he remembered it.

The little swatch of cloth in his pocket. The one he had found on the dirt floor of the chicken coop early that morning. With his thumb and forefinger, he reached inside his pocket, pinched the small piece of cloth and brought it out. Looked at it. He knew instantly what it was about Jake's hat that bothered him.

The hat band. The small strip of cloth that circled the hat. Like a ribbon. The little piece of cloth he had extracted from his pocket matched Jake's hat band, he thought. Same ribbed material. Same color.

But that didn't necessarily prove anything. He closed his eyes and let the image of Jake's hat come to mind. There had been a ragged edge on the hat band. He was sure of it. Or was he? His mind had been so foggy when he had seen Jake's hat, he might have imagined it. There must be hundreds of hats that were decorated with that same kind of band. For all he knew, Paul himself may have owned a hat with a torn band.

"What have you got there?" Anita said when she came back in the room carrying a bowl of warm water. A towel and wash cloth were draped over her arm. She set the bowl down beside the family bible on the low table next to the bed.

"Just a piece of cloth." He held it up for her to see. "Recognize it?"

She took the two-inch strip of material from him, examined it.

"Looks like a piece of ribbon to me."

"Yeah, that's what I thought. Does it belong to you?"

"No. I don't have any tan-colored ribbons."

"How about Paul? Maybe it belonged to him."

"He didn't wear ribbons," she smiled, cocking her head quizzically. "I don't understand."

"I meant maybe he had a string tie or a hat with a band that matched this."

"Yeah. He might have a hat with a band that color. Why?"

"I found this out in the chicken coop, near Paul's body."

Her eyes widened.

"Let me check. I'll be right back." She went to Paul's room, returned a moment later with a straw-colored hat. Bolt took the hat from her, placed the scrap of ribbon on top of the band circling Paul's hat. Same material. Same color. It was damned close. But not close enough. The band on Paul's hat was a good quarter of an inch wider than the scrap. It was a shade darker, too. Besides, Paul's hat band wasn't torn.

"Anita, I think this piece of ribbon was torn off of something during the struggle when Paul was killed."

He looked into her eyes, saw the pain. "There was a struggle, you know," he said gently. "The ground showed signs of a scuffle."

Her body shuddered with the thought.

"Paul may have grabbed for anything he could during that struggle. I'm almost positive that this little piece of cloth belongs to the man who murdered Paul. If we can find out who it belongs to, we'll know for sure who killed your brother."

"It's a common ribbon used for hat bands. But, I think you're right. If we can find out where it came from, we'll know . . . who killed my brother. I'm sure it came from one of the Guthrie brothers," she said, dismissing the subject. "Now, I've got to get that shirt off of you and get you cleaned up."

She took the piece of cloth from Bolt and stuck it inside the cover of the family bible that was on the nearby table. She dunked the washcloth into the bowl of warm water, wrung out the excess water and applied it to the back of Bolt's shirt where it stuck to raw wounds. She dabbed at it again and again until she was gradually able to peel the shirt free of the skin. Bolt grimaced as she gently pried the material loose.

Carefully, she removed the shirt and looked at the ugly furrows on his back. The gaping dirt-embedded wounds on the elbows and upper arms made her stomach turn.

"How bad is it?" Bolt asked.

"Bad enough. But if I can get all that dirt cleaned out, I think you'll be all right in a few days."

"Nothing seems to be broken, at least." Bolt felt his wrists and arms, the ribs that were bruised.

She washed his face first, dabbing at the dirt that was lodged in open cuts. Then she soaked the dried blood that matted his hair. He flinched when she touched the lump on the back of his head. She set the washcloth down for a moment, walked across the room to a cupboard where she poured an amber liquid into a glass. She came back and handed the glass to him.

"Here, drink this. Papa's special brandy. Might help the pain."

"Thanks." He took a healthy slug of the brandy.

She continued washing the dirt from his raw wounds, picking out tiny rocks from the long scratches on his back, scrubbing dried blood from his skin.

"Jake and I decided to get married Friday morning," she said casually as she scoured the dirt from his hands.

"Are you sure, Anita? Sure that you want to marry Jake?"

"Yes. He's good to me, Bolt. He loves me and I love him."

"You deserve to be happy. I hope you will be."

He wouldn't tell her how he felt about Jake. It wouldn't be fair to her. It was really none of his business anyway. He just didn't want to see her hurt. He figured Jake was marrying her for her money. At least that's the impression he got when he overheard their conversation earlier. Also, he had a gut feeling that Jake was somehow involved in Paul's death. He hoped he was wrong. For Anita's sake. What was it the Guthrie brothers had said? The crazy one. Clay. Something about the Guthrie boys owning the Pike ranch after Jake and Anita were married. Something wasn't right there, but he couldn't quite put his finger on it. No need to alarm the woman. She wouldn't believe him anyway. Suspicions weren't facts.

"Well, you look a mite better than you did," she said. She stepped back and looked at him. "I've never seen anybody so dirty in my life. You look almost human again. Now, lie down so I can pull your trousers off."

"But. . . ."

"Come on. That's the only way I can wash the other half of you."

He eased himself back down on the bed, trying to protect the places where he hurt. He unbuttoned his pants, slid them down over his hips. She pulled the trousers the rest of the way. She fumbled with his shorts, sliding them down his legs. Self consciously, Bolt rolled over on his side, facing away from her.

"Your bottom is black and blue all over, but at least you're not cut there. Stay right there while I wash you."

She grabbed the washcloth and scrubbed his backside, dried him, then rolled him onto his back. Delicately, she washed his genitals.

Her warm touch felt good. His manhood twitched, began to grow. Damn thing had a mind of its own. He wanted to pull the covers up over him. He wanted to crawl into a hole and disappear. Instead, he grew bigger and harder. He wondered what Anita was thinking.

She pretended not to notice his erection, but she couldn't keep her eyes off of it. She was fascinated by its size, its length. Bolt's penis was so much bigger than Jake's.

Sex was something new in her life. She had only made love once and that had been with Jake the night before, although it seemed more like a month ago. The experience had been somewhat disappointing because it was all over so quick. She wondered what it would feel like to have such a big one inside her. She wondered if it would fit. She felt her loins twitch, felt the warmth of desire stir inside her. Her panties dampened with a warm sticky substance that she didn't understand. It hadn't been like that with Jake.

Realizing that she shouldn't be thinking such thoughts about another man so close to her wedding, she dried him quickly and turned away.

"I'll get you a pair of Papa's pajamas. You're probably cold."

"No, I'm hot."

Her face flushed crimson. She hoped Bolt didn't notice.

"Are you hungry?" she asked when she brought the pajamas.

"Yes, I am."

"Good. I've fixed a nice supper." She helped him into the pajamas then went to the kitchen to dish up their food.

She served Bolt's food on a tray. She pulled her chair up next to the bed and balanced a plate on her knees.

"Jake wondered if you wanted to buy the ranch," Anita said when they had finished eating.

"I'm not sure yet. I want to look at a couple of places before I decide. I'm not even sure it'll be in Dodge City."

"I understand. I don't know why Jake's in such a hurry for me to sell this place."

"I thought you wanted to sell it."

"I do, but I don't like being rushed into it. I think it would be better to wait until we get back."

"Where are you going?"

"To Cheyenne. Jake wants to go there and get his money out of the bank. We don't know where we'll settle, but we'll have to come back here anyway. At least long enough for me to clear things up, get my things out of the house."

"When are you getting married?"

"At eleven Friday morning. That will give us time to catch the afternoon stage coach to Cheyenne."

"I appreciate you taking care of me. I should be up and about by tomorrow. By Friday at least. I'll be on my way as soon as I'm able."

"You'll stay right here in bed until you're better. Besides I want you to stay long enough for the wedding. I don't have any family now, but I'd like you to be here as a friend."

"I'll be here for the wedding. I wouldn't miss it."

"I'm glad. You can stay in bed all day tomorrow. I have to go into town in the morning. I have a lot to do, but you should be all right while I'm gone. I have to go to the bank and get my money out. I want to do a little shopping, too."

"Why do you have to get money from the bank?" He knew why, but he was trying to make her realize what she was doing.

"Well, Jake wants me to draw all my money out of the bank. He'll get his money when we get to Cheyenne. That way we'll have it all with us wherever we go."

"Seems to me it'd be safer in the bank until you actually need it. No telling what you'll run into. Not all people are honest, you know."

"You're probably right, but Jake thinks it will be handier if we have all the money with us."

Bolt dropped the subject. God, couldn't she see what that bastard Jake was doing? He guessed not. People were funny that way. They tended to see only what they wanted to see.

"You look tired, Bolt. You'd better get some sleep now and I'll see you in the morning."

She got up and pushed her chair against the wall. She pulled the covers up around Bolt.

"Thanks, Anita, for taking care of me. I feel better."

"You look better, too. I hope you'll be able to sleep. If you need anything during the night, don't hesitate to call me."

He was sure he would need something, but he wouldn't call her.

\* \* \* \* \* \* \* \* \* \*

"The wedding's set for Saturday morning," Jake lied.

"Can't you make it any sooner?" Wes grumbled. He was impatient. Jake had assured him that he had taken Bolt to the sheriff's office and testified that he had seen Bolt murder Anita's brother. He felt relieved about that, but he wouldn't be happy until he had the Pike land deed in his hands.

"No. You know how women are. She wants to buy a wedding dress, make her preparations for the wedding. She's still hurting over her brother's death, too."

"Shit! The land office is probably closed Saturday. That'll mean it'll be Monday before she can sign the deed over."

"Sorry, but that's the best I could do." By Monday morning, he'd be long gone. And, the sheriff would be looking for the Guthrie boys by Friday afternoon. He'd take care of that right before he and Anita boarded the stage.

\* \* \* \* \* \* \* \* \* \*

Anita left the house shortly after ten Thursday morning. She had checked Bolt's wounds before she left. Bolt was still pretty sick, but he was improving. He said he wouldn't need anything while she was gone.

On her way to town in her horse and carriage, she thought about the things that were happening in her life. She was full of grief over Paul's death, and yet she was happy and excited about her wedding to Jake. She forced herself not to think about the excitement she had felt with Bolt. That was something she had thought about all night. She sensed that Bolt didn't particularly like Jake, but he was like her brother that way. Suspicious of people. Thinking Jake wasn't good enough for her.

She felt lost with Paul and her father gone. They were the only family she had. She had never known her mother. She had died when Anita was a tiny baby. She felt lucky to have Jake to take care of her. He might have some faults, but he would be a good husband. They had never talked about having children, but she wanted a big family. Strange, she thought, but she didn't really know much about Jake.

The main street of Dodge City was lined with horses and buggies. A hundred of them, at least. That was normal for this boom town. Ladies dressed in fine gowns strolled along the boardwalks, parasols draped over their arms. They seemed to enjoy looking in store windows, stopping to chat with friends. The men gathered in small groups in front of the false fronts, discussing cattle prices or politics, she supposed.

It was a beautiful crisp day. She felt the autumn breeze tug at her bonnet, ruffle her hair.

"Good morning, Miss Pike," said the man standing behind the teller's window at the bank.

"Good morning, Mr. Davis. Beautiful day, isn't it?"

"Yes indeed."

"I'd like to draw my money out of the bank, please."

"All of it?"

"Yes, please."

"Just a moment. I'll check your account." He returned a few moments later. "Miss Pike, I'll need your brother's signature, too, because your account, your father's money, was left to both of you."

"My brother's dead."

"I'm sorry to hear that. Just a minute and I'll draw up a draft. You'll have to sign an affadavit about your brother's death. Now, how much cash will you need?"

He returned with a stack of bills, counted them out in front of her. She signed the affadavit and a receipt. She took the money. He handed her a draft for forty-nine thousand dollars. She put the cash and draft in her purse.

"Thank you, Mr. Davis."

She walked to the general store, where she picked out a yellow and white dress that would serve as her wedding dress. Yellow was her favorite color. It made her feel cheerful. She picked out two long yellow candles and a vase that would hold flowers.

She went back to her carriage, clutching her purse in her hands. She felt uncomfortable with that much money in her possession. Fear gripped her. That was all the money she had in the world. Of course the draft was made out in her name. Still, she was afraid of losing it or having it stolen. People were killed for a lot less money.

She looked around to see if anyone was watching her. As she rode off, she cringed whenever a man riding a horse went by her. She imagined that she was being followed, but she wasn't.

By the time she got home, she was trembling, partly with fear and partly with the relief of being home safe with her money intact. Inside the house, she took the money and the draft out of her purse, glanced around for a safe hiding place. Finally, she went to her bedroom and hid the money under the mattress.

She would be glad when she and Jake were married. Then she wouldn't have to worry anymore.

# CHAPTER SIXTEEN

"What in the hell happened to you?" Tom Penrod asked Friday morning.

"It's a long story," Bolt said in their hotel room.

Bolt had slept fitfully the night before, after sleeping Thursday away. He woke up several times, his body aching with the bruises. When he did sleep, he had haunting dreams. Dreams of terror. Dreams of death. Frustrating dreams of love and unfulfilled desire.

When he awoke this morning, he was stiff all over, but most of the pain was gone. Anita had laid out fresh clothes for him. Paul's probably. After he dressed, he shared a quick cup of coffee with Anita. He asked her if she had a pistol he could borrow and she had given him one from her father's drawer. She had also given him her father's gold pocket watch. Said she wanted him to have it.

He assured her he would be back in time for the wedding and asked her to tell Jake that he would have the money for the ranch when he returned. He got his horse from the stable and left in a hurry.

He had a lot to do before eleven o'clock.

Tom looked at Bolt's battered face, held his hand up in the air.

"Don't bother to explain," he said. "I know it was a woman. And a jealous husband, I'll bet."

"Tom, I've got a favor to ask of you."

"It figures."

"I haven't got time to explain. I want you to go to get the sheriff. Bring him out to the Pike ranch at eleven o'clock. It's important or I wouldn't ask."

"Yeah, I know. I'll be there."

"Don't be late. I hope we're in time to stop a wedding."

\* \* \* \* \* \* \* \* \* \*

"Another day we should be in Dodge City," said Will Atterbury.

The three men huddled around a campfire. A cold night breeze flapped their jackets.

"I sure hope Bolt's there," said a shivering Bob Steckley.

"He's there," said Chad Fisher, stroking his thin moustache. "That's what his whore told me. Said he was going to Dodge after stopping to see his father in Ellsworth. She was telling the truth. I made sure of that. But we've already lost two days back there in Ellsworth. It beats me how you two dumbbells could lose track of him so quickly."

"We saw him go in the church," said Will defensively. "He just never came out."

"I don't want to hear your excuses any more."

"But, he's slippery. I told you that."

Chad was moody. Had been most of the trip. He had developed a real hatred for Jared Bolt. A respect, too. He had to admire a man who could give him the slip so many times. Will was right, of course. Bolt was slippery. But that only made Chad more determined to get Bolt. Dead or alive. It didn't much matter to him any more. One way or the other, sooner or later, he would get Bolt. He always got what he went after.

\* \* \* \* \* \* \* \* \* \*

Bolt was not thinking about the three bounty hunters who had been after him in Abilene, who had stalked him to Ellsworth. He had other things on his mind now.

He was on his way to settle a score with the Guthrie brothers.

He rode his horse as far as he dared. He was five hundred yards from the Guthrie house when he stopped, dismounted and tied his horse to a tree. He would walk the rest of the way. The house was just beyond the next rise, out of sight. He drew his pistol out of its holster, checked it, and slipped it back in. He flattened himself against the ground and began crawling up to the top of the rise. Stiff, sore muscles ached as he pulled himself along. His head throbbed with pain. His shirt rubbed against the raw wounds on his back.

He headed for a group of large boulders that perched atop the small hill. He inched along the hard ground, dragging himself along on bruised elbows. The pain was excruciating. When he reached the top, he tucked in close to the boulders, keeping his silhouette low. The morning sun had already warmed the rock formations and the heat felt good on his back.

From his vantage point, he could see the Guthrie house, the land surrounding it. Two of the brothers were in the front yard. They were dipping water from a large watering trough. There was no sign of the third brother.

Bolt crouched low, watching them fill their pails. They were like sitting ducks. Easy targets if he were closer. He wouldn't risk a shot from this distance. He might be able to hit one of them from where he was, but it would be sheer luck to get the second one.

When the third bucket was filled, the two men carried them off. One brother struggled with two buckets, the water sloshing back and forth, spilling over the top. The other man carried only one bucket. They walked around the back of the house, out of sight.

Bolt saw his chance to move in on them. He scrambled down the gentle slope, his boots kicking up the dry loose dirt. He made a dash for the watering trough, ducked down behind it. He edged down to the end where a tall pump stood.

Bolt reached into his pocket and extracted the pocket watch Anita had given him. Ten twenty. Not much time left before Anita's wedding. The minutes dragged by. Dammit, where in hell were they? He drew his pistol, cocked it. And then he waited. Waited and thought. His eyes turned to cold agates when he recalled the torture he had suffered at the hands of the Guthrie brothers.

Finally, he heard voices. Growing louder. The brothers were returning. Bolt raised up slightly, peeked over the edge of the trough. He saw them coming toward him. The closest man, the taller of the two, carried two empty buckets. The other brother, the one with a limp, useless hand, carried only one. Eddie and Clay.

He waited until they were five feet away before he stood up, his pistol ready.

"What the hell. . . ." said the startled Clay. He looked at the barrel of the pistol aimed at him, his mouth hanging open with shock.

"You boys want to come into town with me? Answer some questions?"

"Fuck you," said Clay, reaching for his pistol.

Bolt fired, hit him square between the eyes. Blood blossomed from the gaping hole in the middle of his forehead. Clay's eyes widened in surprise. He staggered two steps forward and toppled head first into the trough. His limp body hung over the edge, his head completely submerged. The water crimsoned with his blood. The back of his head was gone. Gobs of sticky brain matter floated briefly in the reddening water before sinking.

"You fucking bastard!" Eddie shouted. He drew his pistol a split second after Bolt fired at Clay.

In one smooth motion, Bolt twisted his body around and shot at Eddie.

Eddie fired, as well. Too late. He was already half way to the ground, his lungs ripped to shreds. Eddie's stray bullet spanged against an empty bucket.

Blood gushed from his chest. A dark circular stain spread across his shirt. He collapsed on the ground, his neck twisted at a grotesque angle. He tried to speak, but he had no voice. Pink foam gurgled up in his throat, spilled out of his crooked mouth. He gasped for the breath that didn't come. Desperately, he clutched at his chest, trying to force the precious air inside. His eyes glazed over with a vacant stare.

And then everything went quiet. Too quiet.

Bolt looked up at the house, expecting to see Wes Guthrie come dashing out the door. Nothing. Maybe he wasn't there. Surely he would come out shooting if he was inside. Bolt ducked down and waited.

Precious minutes ticked away. One minute. Two minutes. Three, four. Five minutes. Still nothing. Wes didn't show.

Bolt could wait no longer. He had to find out if Wes was inside the house. He ran in a zigzag pattern across the yard. When he was twenty feet away from the house, movement caught his eye. A curtain at the window moved slightly. He hurled himself headlong at the ground. Aimed his pistol at the window.

The curtain was motionless.

\* \* \* \* \* \* \* \* \* \*

Jake arrived promptly at ten thirty. He heard the distant shots. Scratched his head.

Anita greeted him at the door.

Radiant in her long yellow frock. A wide white band, embroidered with delicate yellow flowers, circled her tiny waist. A yellow ribbon held her hair in place. Dark curls fell softly to her shoulders. Satin slippers, dyed to match her outfit, peeked out beneath her gown.

"You're beautiful, Anita."

"Thank you, Jake. I'm so nervous."

She looked up at him, her eyes glittering with excitement. He was a good twelve inches taller than she. Jake was handsome in a dark brown gabardine suit, a white shirt and brown tie. He removed his hat when he entered the room. He leaned down, kissed her briefly.

"Are you all ready for the big event?"

"I'm ready. Where's the preacher?"

"He'll be along in a few minutes. Don't worry. I've arranged everything."

"I know you have. I'm just nervous."

"There's no need to be. Everything's going to work out fine."

Jake was able to conceal his own edginess behind a mask of outer calm. The only thing on his mind was Anita's money. He wanted to be assured that she had drawn her father's money from the bank. But he wouldn't ask just yet. Too obvious.

"How's Bolt this morning?" he asked. "Where is he?"

"He's sore and stiff, but he's much better. He went to town to get his money. He said for me to tell you that he wanted to buy the ranch and that he'd be back with the money before the wedding."

Anita didn't detect the smirk of satisfaction that crossed Jake's face.

"Good. Everything's working out fine. The stage coach leaves at two this afternoon. I've arranged for us to have a special wedding dinner at Delmonico's. Champagne and all. We'll ride the stage as far as Cimmoron this evening. It stops there overnight." He'd take Anita as far as Cheyenne before he dumped her penniless. It would take her a little time to realize that he was gone. It would take her even longer to return to Dodge City. By the time she got back home, he would be in California, living the good life.

"Oh, Jake, I'm so excited. You make me very happy."

"Have you got your bags packed?"

"Yes. My two bags are in the hallway. I've got a small satchel in my room."

"I'll put them in the carriage while we're waiting."

They walked to the hallway together.

Jake handed his hat to her, then lifted the heavy bags. He turned and carried them outside.

Anita entered her room, looked at the carpetbag on the bed. It was still open. She hadn't wanted to put her money in it until the very last minute. She felt safer now that Jake was here. She set Jake's hat on the dresser so she could get the money from under her mattress. She noticed that a small piece of the hat band was missing from the brown hat.

It didn't register until she had taken a couple of steps. She turned and stared at the hat. She grabbed it up in her hands. Her stomach began to churn. Shock set in as she gazed wide-eyed at the jagged edge of the torn band.

She ran to her father's room, snatched the small piece of ribbon from inside the bible. The jagged edges lined up perfectly. Her heart skipped a beat. Her hands began to tremble. What did it mean?

She tried to calm herself. She tried to think clearly. There had to be a logical explanation. The only thing Jake's hat proved was that he was in the chicken coop. But she knew better than that. He'd never been anyplace except inside the house. But that didn't mean that Jake was Paul's murderer, like Bolt said. It couldn't mean that.

She walked back to her room slowly, trying to sort out the confusion in her mind. She sat on the edge of the bed staring blankly at her folded hands in her lap. She knew one thing for a fact. Jake had been in the chicken coop when Paul was murdered.

She knew in her heart that Jake had murdered Paul.

She heard the front door open and close. Jake was back in the house.

Panic gripped her. She knew she was alone with a murderer! Her face blanched white. Her legs turned rubbery when she stood up. She wanted to run outside. She wanted to scream. She thought about getting her brother's pistol, but she wasn't a very good shot.

"Anita?" Jake called.

"I'll be right there." She wouldn't have time to get the pistol.

Where was the preacher? Where was Bolt? She was frightened to death to be alone with Jake.

"Anita, what's wrong?" he said when he saw her. "You look sick."

"Just nerves," she said. She couldn't bear to look him in the eye.

"You'll be all right when it's all over with." He started to put his arm around her. She ducked away from him, sat on the couch.

Jake slapped his hands together.

"Well, I guess everything's set," he said, a bit too loud. "Oh, by the way, Anita, did you get your money out of the bank?" He had to know.

She shot him a look.

So that was his scheme. He wanted her money. Her father's money. How could she have been so blind? That explained the quick wedding, the sale of the ranch. But it didn't explain Paul's death. Or did it? Paul was against their marriage. He didn't like Jake at all. Hadn't liked him from the beginning. And Paul had kicked Jake out of the house the night before the murder.

"Yes. Well, not exactly," she lied. "I went to the bank yesterday morning and arranged to get the money. They said it would take time to get the money together. Mr. Davis said he would have it all ready before noon today. We can pick it up when we go into town."

That was good enough for Jake. He didn't anticipate any trouble getting the money if Mr. Davis said he'd have it ready. He pulled his pocket watch out of his vest, checked the time.

"Twenty more minutes. The preacher should be here by now."

Anita didn't think she could wait another twenty minutes. She got up, walked to the window and pulled the curtain aside. Her eyes searched the road for the preacher. For Bolt. She released the sheer curtain, walked back to her spot on the couch. Jake sat down beside her. She jumped up and walked to the table she had arranged for their wedding. Yellow candles flanked a huge bouquet of fresh-picked flowers.

"How do you like the flowers?" she asked nervously.

"They're beautiful, like you." He walked toward her.

"I baked a wedding cake, too," she said quickly.

She ran her hands along the smooth surface of the table so that Jake wouldn't see them tremble. When he got close to her she moved away again.

"Would you like some coffee, Jake?" She didn't know what she was saying. She just had to keep busy until someone came.

"No thanks. Sit down, will you."

She chose a chair that faced the fireplace. At least he couldn't sit down next to her. Why did the time drag so? It must be eleven o'clock by now. But she knew it wasn't. It seemed like an hour since Jake had come back into the house.

She heard a horse approaching outside.

"What time is it? she asked.

"A quarter till eleven."

\* \* \* \* \* \* \* \* \* \*

Bolt checked the watch again. Fifteen minutes till eleven. He cursed the time that was slipping away. He had to get back to Anita's before it was too late. He was on the porch of the Guthrie house, hugging the wall beside the door.

He knew Wes was inside. He listened, heard nothing. He held his cocked pistol in his right hand, tried the door handle with his left. It was locked. He checked the windows and then brought his leg up, jammed it hard against the door. The door flew open with the impact. He dropped down on his haunches, eyes scanning for movement, form.

Inside, the house was dark, quiet.

No one was there.

## CHAPTER SEVENTEEN

Bolt swung the door all the way open. He went inside, pistol cocked. Sunlight filtered through the door, reflected off his pistol as he stalked around the room. He checked behind the furniture. The livingroom was a mess. The tattered couch with its grimy stains, was littered with newspapers. Empty glasses and beer bottles were strewn over tables and the floor.

He moved quickly to the next room, paused, his back against the door frame. The kitchen was even filthier than the livingroom. Dirty dishes covered the table, lined the countertop. The stench of spoiled food drifted to his nostrils. Carefully, he moved into the room.

A cat jumped off the counter. Bolt whirled around, pointed his pistol at the sound, started to squeeze the trigger. He saw the cat and sucked in a deep breath. Adrenalin dumped into his bloodstream. His heart was beating a mile a minute. He relaxed his trigger finger.

He went back through the livingroom to a bedroom on the other side of the house. Again he stood against the door frame so he could scan both rooms at once. He knew Wes had to be in there someplace. He had seen the shadow at the window just before the curtain stopped moving.

Just as he was about to enter the bedroom, he heard a noise. He stood very still and listened. It was coming from outside. Hoofbeats pounding the ground.

The sound grew louder as the horse came closer to the house. Bolt dashed to the bedroom window, pulled the curtain aside, just as the horse sped by. Bolt saw the ugly scar on the side of Wes Guthrie's face as he flashed by. A second later Wes was out of sight as the horse rounded the house.

Bolt dashed through the house and out the front door. He was in time to see Wes go around a bend on the dirt road that lead to town. He aimed his pistol at the moving target, but knew he was too far away. If he hurried, Bolt still had a chance at Wes. The road, he knew, went south for a ways and then looped around close to the place where Bolt had tied his horse.

He dashed across the yard, past the bloody bodies of Eddie and Clay. He scrambled up the slope, made it to the top of the rise. He could see the dirt road just below him.

He darted to his horse, a few feet away, jerked the reins from the tree and mounted him, kicked him into action. He heard the pounding hooves coming in his direction. He was in time.

He reined back, waited until the timing was exactly right, then barreled out toward the road. When Wes went by, he cut onto the road, came up slightly behind his prey.

"Hold it right there, Guthrie, or you're dead."

Wes turned his head. He stared down the barrel of Bolt's pistol. Wes started to go for his gun, heard the click of Bolt's hammer gear. He knew he wouldn't have a chance. He hauled back on the reins.

Both horses came to a stop.

"I need some answers and I need them fast. Who killed Paul Pike?"

"Fuck you, Bolt."

Bolt rammed his horse close to Guthrie, rammed his pistol barrel under the man's chin.

"It was Brady, I know. I just want to hear you say it, asshole."

"Jesus. Yair. Brady. He — he did the cuttin."

"You help him?"

Bolt pushed upward underneath the man's chin, forcing Wes' head back. His neck muscles tautened.

"Hell, we was all there. That crazy fucking Clay. He — he cut off the boy's hands. I don't hold with that. Bolt, Christ, I can't breathe. I can't talk."

Bolt moved his pistol barrel slightly. Wes' head came back down. He sat his horse stiffly, one eye on that cocked hammer. Sweat dribbled into his eyes.

"Why'd you rub the boy out?"

"It was Jake. I mean, he had to marry the gal. To get the ranch. Pike didn't go fer it. It — it was his idea."

"You lying sack of shit! You boys wanted that water. Thought you could muscle that girl if her brother was face down under six feet of dirt."

Wes showed the whites of his eyes as Bolt pushed his Adam's apple hard with the pistol barrel.

"Yair. We needed the water, all right."

"You and your brothers got all the water they're gonna get."

Bolt shot a hand to Wes' holster, drew the man's pistol. He tucked it in his waistband, backed his horse away.

"You ride on ahead real careful, Guthrie. If you twitch an eyebrow, some holes are going to open up in your hide. You dumb sonofabitch, Jake was doublecrossing you boys."

Wes' horse stepped gingerly forward. Bolt rode close, to the side. His face was granite, a single muscle twitching along the jawline. It took all of his willpower not to blow Guthrie's head into the next county.

"What were you payin' Jake, Guthrie?"

"Thousand dollars."

"Hell, he stood to get more than that from the Pike woman. More like fifty."

Wes made a disgusting noise with his mouth.

"I'll kill him, the dirty double-crossing. . . ."

"You'll shit," Bolt said drily. "Keep moving. One twitch, son. Just one."

Wes Guthrie didn't twitch.

\* \* \* \* \* \* \* \* \* \*

"The preacher's here," said Jake from the window.

Anita's knees went weak with relief. Her body began to shake. It wasn't over yet, but at least she wouldn't be alone with Jake. She wouldn't marry him. But where was Bolt?

She had the door open before the preacher reached the porch.

"Come in, Reverend Price."

Reverend Price was a short man with a slight limp. The sun bounced off a shiny bald spot on the top of his head. The sparse hair he possessed was gray, neatly trimmed. He wore a black suit, carried a bible tucked under one arm. A gold watch fob dangled from his vest pocket.

"Lovely day for a wedding," he said, "and you make a lovely bride."

"Thank you. Please make yourself comfortable," Anita said, waving him to the couch.

The preacher exchanged greetings with Jake, shook his hand. He sat down on the divan, his legs clamped together, his feet planted firmly on the floor. He set the bible on the short-legged table in front of him.

"Who else will be here for the wedding?"

"A friend of ours is to be here," Anita replied.

"That's fine," said the prim preacher. "You need a witness, you know."

Anita could have kissed the elderly minister. That meant that she could stall until Bolt arrived. Bolt would help her. She managed to carry on a light conversation with Reverend Price while Jake paced back and forth from the couch to the open window. At the window, he pulled the curtain back, scanned the road for a sign of Bolt. He pulled his pocket watch out, checked the time, then jammed the gold watch back in his pocket. Anita watched Jake perform the ritual several times.

Finally, Jake turned from the window.

"I'd like to go ahead with the wedding, Reverend Price. It's eleven o'clock and it's obvious that our friend has been detained."

Anita froze in her chair, her hands gripping the sculptured arms of the chair tightly.

"I'm sorry, sir, that wouldn't be proper. I need the signature of the witness on the marriage certificate. Otherwise, the marriage wouldn't be legal."

"Can't you get someone to sign it later? We have to catch the afternoon stage coach. We have just barely enough time to eat a wedding dinner before we go. I'll pay you extra if you can find someone to sign it later."

"Oh, no, sir, I couldn't do that." He sat up a little straighter in the chair, as if to emphasize his authority.

Jake didn't have to wait any longer. He heard the hoof beats that signalled Bolt's arrival.

"Jake?" Bolt shouted from outside. "Jake Brady! Come out here!"

Jake peered out the window, saw Bolt and Guthrie climb from their horses.

"It's Bolt," said Jake, "and he's got Wes Guthrie with him."

"I didn't know you knew Wes Guthrie," said Anita accusingly.

"I've seen him around," he said lamely. "I'll go see if I can help out."

Anita saw Jake touch a bulge in his clothing before he opened the door.

When Jake walked outside, Anita ran to her room, jerked a dresser drawer open. She rummaged through soft filmy lingerie until she found what she was looking for. Her brother's pistol. She knew it was loaded, ready to shoot. She was scared to death of guns. But she had hidden it after Paul had been killed. She had shot at targets a couple of times because her father thought she should know how to use one, but she was a terrible shot. She held the pistol in the folds of her skirt, ran to the front door.

Other horses approached. Tom Penrod was in the lead. Behind him were Sheriff Hall and two deputies. Tom brought his horse to a halt, jumped down and stood near Bolt. The sheriff and his men hung back, watching.

Bolt looked at the house, saw Anita standing in the doorway.

"Anita! Stay right where you are! Wes Guthrie has something to tell you!" Bolt's voice was loud, carried authority in its tone. He turned to Wes. "Go ahead, Wes. Tell her who killed her brother, Paul."

"Jake Brady," he mumbled, his eyes fixed on the ground. His voice was barely audible.

"Louder, Guthrie! She can't hear you! Who killed her brother!"

"Jake Brady killed him!" he yelled.

"You dirty sonofabitch!" Jake spat.

Jake drew his pistol, fired. The bullet whizzed from the barrel before anyone could react. Guthrie's body jerked from the impact. Blood gushed from his chest. Chunks of flesh splattered in all directions.

Bits of flesh spattered on Bolt's pants. Wes crumpled to the ground.

Jake turned quickly, aimed at Bolt.

Another shot rang out.

Jake felt the sting, grabbed his right forearm. His pistol dropped to the ground. He looked down, saw blood trickle from the hole in his sleeve, through the fingers that clutched it. His eyes widened in surprise. He looked at the other men to see who had shot him. He knew it wasn't Bolt.

Bolt's eyes darted to the doorway. He saw Anita standing there, a smoking pistol clutched in both hands.

Sheriff Hall moved in and grabbed Jake by his good arm, kicked Jake's gun out of reach.

Wes Guthrie moaned on the ground.

"You double crossed me, Jake," Wes gasped. His head fell to his shoulder. His eyes filmed over as death invaded him.

Anita ran out and threw her arms around Bolt.

"I'm so glad you're here. I was so scared."

He looked at her sadly. "I'm sorry, Anita. That things turned out this way."

"I found out before you got here. It was Jake's hat! His hat band! It had a piece torn off!" She was hysterical.

Jake glared at her. He had no idea what she was talking about. But he knew that his plan had blown up in his face.

Sheriff Hall motioned for his deputies. "Get a tourniquet around his arm."

"Why bother?" said Slocum, the deputy.

Hall ignored the remark, turned to the wounded man.

"You'll get a fair trial, Brady. For Paul Pike's death. And this Guthrie man."

Slocum and the other deputy, Peter Stamps, jerked Jake's shirt tail from his trousers, tore a strip from the bottom. Stamps held Brady's arm while Slocum wound the cloth around the arm above the bullet wound. He cinched it up, tighter than needed, tied a quick knot.

"Get on your horse," Hall ordered Jake.

Jake glanced at the sheriff, saw the pistol. Slowly, he mounted his horse. Sheriff Hall retrieved his horse, climbed atop it and pulled a rifle from a scabbard. He lined his horse up directly behind Brady, ordered his deputies to bring their horses up on either side of Jake's horse. Hall turned to Bolt.

"I'll send the undertaker out to take care of the body."

Bolt put his arm around Anita's shoulder. Tom stood next to Bolt, watched as the four men rode off. When they were out of sight, Tom spoke.

"I'll get the horses, Bolt."

"Anita, this is my friend, Tom Penrod. Be back out in a minute, Tom." He turned and led Anita to the house.

Reverend Price stood in the doorway.

"I guess you won't be needing me now, Miss Pike."

Anita had forgotten about the preacher.

"No. Thank you for coming. I'll pay you, of course."

"No need."

Bolt reached in his pocket and drew out a bill, handed it to the elderly preacher.

"May God bless you," said the gray-haired man to Anita as he walked away.

"Well, it's all over with," Bolt said inside the house.

"Yes. Thank God."

She sat down on the couch, put her head in her hands and began to sob softly.

He let her cry. Finally, she relaxed and looked up at him.

"Oh, Bolt, I'm so alone now."

"It won't always be that way. You're young and pretty. You'll meet the right man some day."

"I don't think I could ever trust another man."

"It could have been a lot worse."

"I know. I'm grateful to you." She shuddered when she thought about how close she'd come to marrying Jake.

"Jake was a bad apple, Anita, rotten to the core. He's the lowest kind of man there is. The scum of the earth. He doesn't have a conscience. He'll hang. But not all men are like that. There are a lot of good men. You'll make one of them a good wife."

She sighed deeply.

"You make me feel better."

"I have to go now. Tom's waiting. The undertaker will be out after awhile. Maybe the sheriff. I'll come out this evening to check on you."

"Bolt?"

"Yes?"

"Would you spend the night with me? I don't want to be alone. Not tonight." There was a pleading in her eyes, a desperation.

He looked at her and smiled.

Tom could find his way back.

## CHAPTER EIGHTEEN

"Let me look at that arm," said Sheriff Hall.

It was noon when Hall and his two deputies arrived at the jail with their prisoner. The deputies, Dean Slocum and Peter Stamps, shoved and kicked Jake roughly as they put him in a cell. Frank Hall looked at the wound in Jake's arm, loosened the makeshift tourniquet. The wound began to bleed again.

"We'd better get him to the doctor. The bullet is still in his arm."

"There's no need to fix his arm," pouted Slocum. "He'll hang by morning."

"He'll have a fair trial," said Hall sharply. "It's not human to let a man suffer. Any man. You two take him over to Doc Miley. If Miley wants to keep him there overnight, I'll send Stamps over to spell you. I have to get the undertaker. Send him for the Guthrie boys."

Reluctantly, Slocum and Stamps took the prisoner across the street to Doc Miley.

Even though the doctor gave him plenty of whiskey before he cut into him, Jake's pain didn't stop. With a sharp knife and a probe, Miley dug and gouged, twisted and scraped before he got the bullet out.

Slocum sat on a chair in the corner, a rifle across his lap. A smirk of satisfaction on his lips. Stamps held Jake down while the doctor removed the bullet. Once the bullet was out, Miley poured raw alcohol in the wound to sterilize it. He wrapped layers of gauze around the arm, taped the gauze in place.

Slocum stood up, sauntered over to the operating table.

"Can we take him back to jail now?"

"Not yet. I have to keep an eye on him. Watch for signs of lead poisoning. I'll change the dressing in a couple of hours."

"Shit," said Slocum. He scuffled back over and plopped in the chair.

Stamps returned to the jail while Doc Miley cleaned up the mess. Slocum slouched his tall frame in the chair, resentful that he had to waste his time guarding a prisoner who was going to hang anyway.

"I'm going to eat now," said the doctor. "Be back in a while. Want me to bring anything back?"

Slocum didn't answer.

"I'll be in the back. Call me if you need me." Doc Miley walked through the curtained doorway to his living quarters.

Slocum fidgeted in his chair. It squeaked. Nervous fingers tapped on the rifle. He'd like to pull the trigger. Blow the bastard to hell. Shove the rifle up his ass hole and pull the trigger.

There was little difference between the two men. Each wanted revenge for the lot they'd drawn in life. Either could kill a man and never blink an eye. The only difference between them was that one wore a tin badge.

Jake lay on the table, a blanket tucked up around his neck. He was exhausted from the ordeal of having the bullet gouged from his flesh. He lay perfectly still, his eyes closed. But he wasn't asleep. He heard the frequent squeaking of the chair, the constant clicking of fingernails against metal, the cracking of nervous knuckles. He wished to hell Slocum would leave.

Slocum scuffled across the floor, jabbed a rifle butt in Jake's ribs. Jake flinched.

"Just wanted to keep you alert," Slocum grinned sarcastically. "You wouldn't want to miss the hanging." He jabbed at the ribs again, harder. He swung the rifle around, jammed the barrel against Jake's chin. Slowly, he pushed against it, tipping Jake's head back.

"Would be so easy," he mumbled, his eyes cold steel.

He backed away when the doctor entered the room. He paced to the window, stared out. He wished he had a bottle of whiskey. It would help pass the time.

The doctor unwrapped the gauze, checked the wound, then wound fresh gauze around the arm. He left the room without saying a word.

Slocum sighed. He walked over to the table where the doctor kept a bottle of whiskey for medicinal purposes, picked up the bottle and took a healthy slug. He ambled back to the hard chair against the wall, settled in for a long wait. He tapped his boot against the wooden floor, tapped his fingers against the rifle.

It was almost more than Jake could stand.

Slocum was totally bored with sitting in one place. He stuck a foot out, looped his boot around the leg of a low table. He dragged it toward him, propped his feet on top. He scrooched his body down and leaned back, his head resting on the back of the chair. Finally, his head drooped to his shoulder, his eyes heavy.

Jake could tell the difference. The fidgeting had stopped. The constant creak of the chair had stopped. The sound of fingernails tapping on the rifle was gone. The heavy, repeated sighs changed to a slow even breathing, punctuated by staccato snores.

Jake raised his head. He'd have to move fast. Quietly, he eased himself off the bed, grabbed his shirt and jacket and stole across the floor on tiptoes. A board creaked.

Slocum stirred, his fingers tightening around the rifle. Jake waited. The snoring began again. He turned the door handle, hoped it wouldn't squeak. He pulled the door open, stepped outside, closing the door silently behind him. Once outside, he slipped into his shirt, tucked it into his pants. He put the jacket on.

Jake stepped out on the boardwalk. He forced himself not to run. He needed time to think. He needed a place where he wouldn't be noticed. He kept walking, keeping his head bent, his face concealed from passersby.

A man walking in front of him turned into the Long Branch Saloon. Jake went in behind him, walked to the end of the long bar. He sat down, made himself as unobtrusive as possible. He ordered a whiskey.

His arm ached beneath the bandages. There was only a slight bulge beneath his jacket sleeve. No one would notice it. He propped his arm on the bar top, tried to relieve the pain. He downed the whiskey, ordered another one. He thought about Anita's money. He'd blown it. Bigger'n shit.

He pulled the watch from his pants pocket, where he had stuck it when the doctor removed his vest. Two forty-five. He got an idea. Maybe it wasn't too late to recoup most of the money. Anita had told him that the money would be ready for her by noon. He doubted that she had come back to town yet. It was worth a try.

He downed his drink, walked back out into the bright sunshine. His eyes darted around. Nobody was waiting for him.

"I'm Jake Brady, Anita Pike's husband," he told the bank teller. "My wife took sick earlier. She asked me to pick up the money we were supposed to get."

Mr. Davis stared blankly at him.

"The money was supposed to be ready at noon today," Jake said. The irritation showed in his voice. "Do you have it? I'm in a hurry."

"I'm sorry, Mr. Brady. Miss Pike already picked up her money. Yesterday morning."

Jake was shocked.

"No. She said we was to pick it up today."

"She came in shortly after we opened yesterday. She got her money then."

Jake's face flushed red. He had to struggle to control his temper.

Mr. Davis stepped back. The stench of Jake's whiskey breath was overpowering.

Jake turned and stormed out the door. That cheap little bitch! he thought. She had the money all the time. She lied to him! Well, he had another surprise for her. He'd get her money, even if he had to kill her to get it!

Shit! He didn't even have a horse. His was tied up at the hitchrail in front of the jail. He didn't dare risk going there. Any horse would do. He could rent one from the stable. He needed a gun, too.

Then he remembered what the sheriff had said. The undertaker might still be there. And that bastard Bolt! He might be there, too. Damn! He'd have to wait a while longer. After dark. That way he could be sure she'd be alone, settled in for the night. He'd find her money if it was the last thing he did.

He stalked to the stables, his anger flaring like the pain in his arm.

\* \* \* \* \* \* \* \* \* \*

It was dusk. The undertaker had left hours ago.

Small pink clouds floated across the darkening sky. Anita and Bolt sat on the porch, enjoying the solitude, the quiet. Anita had changed into a simple blue house dress.

The clouds turned salmon, then purple.

They watched the sky till it turned gray, went inside when it turned dark.

"I'm glad you're here, Bolt. My world is all upside down."

"It's tough. Are you feeling better?"

"Some. Are you hungry? I can fix you something to eat."

"Later."

She hung her head. "Jake and I were supposed to have our wedding dinner at Delmonico's," she said wistfully.

"You can't think about such things."

"How about some wedding cake. I've got one that's going to waste."

"I'm glad you're feeling better. Time will heal all wounds. Remember that."

"Time will wound all heels, too," she smiled.

Impulsively, she threw herself in Bolt's arms, pressed her body close to his.

"I'm glad it's all over, Bolt."

"So am I."

"I have to take my money back to the bank in the morning. Will you go with me?"

"Sure."

They finally ate a light supper. Afterwards, they shared a cup of coffee in the kitchen, talked about Anita's future. They didn't mention the gruesome events of the past couple of days.

"I think you should go to bed now," he urged. "I know you're exhausted. Tomorrow's another day."

"I am tired. You must be, too."

She stood up, started for her room. Suddenly, she turned around and stared into Bolt's clear blue eyes.

"Bolt, I want you to sleep in my bed tonight. I want to be loved. I need it."

They came together. Kissed tenderly.

She walked back to the table, picked up the coal oil lamp and led him to her bedroom. She set the lamp on the dresser, turned back the covers on her bed. She opened the window to let the night air in. She reached under the mattress and removed the bundle of money, placed it in the open carpetbag that was on the floor near the head of the bed, on the side away from the window.

They undressed quickly. Bolt placed his gunbelt on top of the carpetbag. Anita crawled in bed, waited for him. She saw that he was ready for her. He walked over to the lantern, started to blow it out.

"Leave it burning. I want to see you." There was a husk to her voice.

Bolt's stalk twitched. He came to her, snuggled into her open arms. He kissed her passionately, rolled over so that his stiff organ was against her warm leg. He took a breast in his hand, squeezed it.

She responded to his kiss by parting her lips, pushing her tongue inside his mouth. Her warm body wriggled against his. Her loins begged to be touched. He rubbed his hand over her smooth flesh, touched her sensitive places.

Her hand traced a path through his hairy chest, down to his flat, firm belly. She explored his body with delicate fingers, pausing to massage his hips, his buttocks, his inner thighs. Her hand brushed against his erection, then grasped it tightly.

She sat up.

"Bolt, I want to see you. I want to look at your . . . your cock."

She faultered over the word.

Bolt's blood surged.

\* \* \* \* \* \* \* \* \* \*

"Three bucks a day," said the stable boy.

Jake Brady handed the money to the tousled haired boy and took the reins of the horse.

He rode to the end of Center Street, turned right on a side road. A block away, he saw a ramshackle bar. He tied his horse to the hitchrail, went inside. The bar smelled of whiskey and cigar smoke, beer and urine. The stench of vomit and sweat mingled with cheap toilet water. Drunks and hardcases stood at the bar, bumping into each other, slopping beer and whiskey. A man spit at a spittoon, missed.

Jake spotted an empty bar stool, elbowed his way through the drunken men.

It would be a good place to kill some time.

Two hours later, Jake staggered out behind the building to relieve himself. He pissed against the building. He was surprised that it was dark already. He had drunk more whiskey than he had intended. But it dulled the ache in his arm and gave him the courage he needed.

Back at the bar, he finished his drink, realized that he still didn't have a pistol. He glanced around the room, spotted a likely candidate. An old man, drunker'n seven dollars, weaved toward the bar. Jake saw the pistol beneath his rumpled, stained jacket. The drunk zigzagged across the room, his body leaning at an angle. Short arms flailed air as the man tried to keep his balance.

Jake staggered toward the drunk, barely able to keep his own balance. He bumped against the man, harder than he planned. He missed his chance. The second time he rammed into the drunk, he grabbed for the man's exposed pistol, drew it smoothly from its holster. It took two attempts before he could jam it into his own belt. The old man never noticed.

"Excuse me," Jake slurred politely, then made his way to the door. Outside, he tried to clear his fogged brain. It was no use. He wished he hadn't had so much to drink. He needed to think clearly.

He mounted the rented horse, rode back through the busy town. He took the dirt road that led to the Pike ranch.

When he got away from the bright lights of the wild town, it took him a few minutes to adjust his eyes to the darkness. There was a half moon. Enough to light his way.

He rode his horse as far as he dared. When he saw the small dim glow of light from the distant house, he pulled back on the reins, climbed down. With the reins in one hand, he stabbed at the shadow of a bush with the other. He looped the reins loosely around the main stalk of the wirey bush.

He was feeling no pain. He had consumed enough whiskey during the afternoon and evening to keep two men drunk for a spell. No food.

With wobbly legs, he staggered toward the soft orange glow. He managed to stay upright, although he stumbled frequently. As he neared the house, something in his fogged mind told him to slow down, walk carefully. He tried to walk on tip-toes which threw him off balance. His arms flailed wildly in the air as he steadied himself.

He was drawn to the light like a summer moth. The last few feet were the hardest to maneuver in his condition. He shuffled his feet forward, inch by inch, until he was against the building. If he was sober, it would be no problem.

He moved over a few inches so that he was directly in front of the open window. With bleary eyes, he looked inside, expecting to see Anita in the livingroom. It wasn't the livingroom he saw. The sight he saw inside the bedroom surprised him, but didn't register fully on his drink-fogged brain.

He tried to force his mind to unscramble the meaning of what he saw. He knew Anita and Bolt were in bed together. He knew they were feeling each other's bodies. As soon as the thought was formed, it drifted away. He couldn't concentrate. He couldn't decipher what he saw.

\* \* \* \* \* \* \* \* \* \*

Neither Bolt nor Anita saw the face at the window. They didn't see the hand on the window ledge that steadied the drunken man outside.

Anita looked lovingly at the shaft she clutched in her hand. It was big, warm, hard. She rolled Bolt over so that he was flat on his back. The soft light from the lantern reflected off the tight shiny flesh of Bolt's erection. Sticky fluid glistened at the slit eye of the mushroom head.

"You're so big. So hard. I can't believe it."

Bolt's stiff organ twitched in her hand.

"You're sweet, Anita. So soft."

His hand moved down to her thighs. She spread her legs slightly, allowing him access to her sex.

She moved her hand around the hard stalk until she had explored every inch of it. Her finger circled the rim of the flared tip. She studied the head, fascinated by the crooked bell shape. She traced a path along the bulging purple veins. She touched the sac that hung underneath. She moved her hand back up the length of the shaft, to the tip, discovered the sticky fluid that oozed out of the small slit. She put her finger tip on it, smeared it around.

She tightened her hand around the thick organ, slid her hand up and down.

Bolt thrust his hips upward, encouraging her.

She dipped her head down to his erection, touched her warm moist lips to the sensitive tip.

Bolt watched her. The lamp light was behind her, silhouetting her head meeting his rigid cock. He was close to orgasm. She pulled off just in time. Another second and it would have been all over.

"You smell so good, Bolt. You taste sweet and fresh."

She had never felt like this before. Desire flooded her loins, caused an uncontrollable twitch inside.

Holding his erection tightly, she bobbed her head back down. Her lips parted, curled around the sensuous head. She accepted his manhood into her mouth, felt the warmth of the bare flesh. It was an odd feeling. An erotic, sensual feeling. Her pussy began throbbing with the spasms of orgasms.

She didn't know what was happening to her. Never before had she felt anything so wonderful.

Bolt's cock slid in and out of her mouth, glistening in the orange light.

\* \* \* \* \* \* \* \* \* \*

Outside the bedroom window, Jake Brady stared in dulled fascination. He watched as Anita took Bolt's large cock into her mouth. He gawked as she bobbed her head up and down the glistening flesh. It made him hot to see her go down on Bolt. He'd never seen anyone do that before. Anita hadn't done that to him. No woman had.

Jake reached down to his crotch, pressed his hand against the hardening bulge in his pants. He could almost feel her lips wrapped around his cock.

Quickly, he began to unbutton his fly.

# CHAPTER NINETEEN

Jake fought the giddiness.

He was so wrapped up in the sexual display beyond the window that the thought of Anita's money didn't enter his mind.

He slid his hand inside his open fly, reached down until he touched the mass of warm flesh. His hand was cold from the night air. It felt good against the warm flesh. He worked the half-hard cock out of the tight confines of his trousers and shorts. He watched Anita suck the man's rod; wrapped his hand around his own cock.

He saw her suck until her cheeks hollowed; felt the pressure on his own staff.

Bolt rolled Anita over on her back, got above her. He lowered himself into position, pushed his erection against her damp portal. He penetrated the warm sheath.

It soaked through to Jake's soggy brain that he had fucked that same girl once. Just a couple of days ago. That was Anita, his Anita. He could feel himself entering Anita. His hand slid slowly down his shaft.

When he had fucked Anita, it hadn't been as good as it was right now. This way, he could see it happening while he was doing it to her.

Bolt pumped into Anita's eager sheath. He pushed his swollen organ deep inside, brought it back out to the tip. He felt her body wriggle beneath him.

Jake pumped his hand up and down his cock, in rhythm with Bolt's strokes. He could see the slick rod slide into her. Could feel it too.

His fogged brain couldn't differentiate between what he was seeing and what he was doing to himself. To him, it was all the same. This was better than it was the other night. Bolt's cock was much bigger than his. Harder, too. Oh, it felt good to have a bigger cock. He had never been able to get a full erection. It had bothered him for a long time. He squeezed his cock. It was only partially hard now. But his other cock, the one he could see, was fully hard.

Bolt moved in and out of Anita with slow, deep strokes. The tight muscles gripped him, pulled him deeper.

"Faster. Faster! Faster!" Jake said to himself.

As if he could read minds, Bolt increased the speed of his stroking.

So did Jake.

Bolt felt his sperm begin to boil, knew he was close to climax. He grabbed Anita, stroked once more.

"Now," he panted.

"Now," husked Jake at the same time.

Bolt spilled his milky seed deep inside her.

Jake splattered his sticky sperm against the building.

Jake moaned.

Loud enough for Bolt and Anita to hear.

Bolt froze, looked at the window.

"What was that?" said Anita.

Bolt saw Jake's face at the window. He pushed Anita off the bed, on the side away from the window. He stretched across the bed, reached for his pistol on top of the carpetbag. It was gone. Anita had bumped it when she tumbled off the bed, knocked it out of reach.

The commotion in the bedroom jolted Jake out of his stupor. He reached for his stolen pistol.

Bolt went for him. Jake stuck his head through the open window, tried to crawl inside. He was half in, half out when Bolt reached him.

Bolt locked his hands together, brought them down in a crashing blow to Jake's head. He dragged Jake inside the room, slammed his fist into Jake's jaw. Jake tumbled backwards, lurched against the wall, ended up on the floor. Fresh blood seeped through his shirt from the bandaged bullet wound.

Bolt lunged at him again. Jake drew his knees up to his chest, kicked out as Bolt approached. His boots caught Bolt in the stomach, sent him hurling across the room, the wind knocked out of him.

Anita crawled along the floor toward Bolt's pistol. Her buttocks bounced up and down. She reached out, snaked the gunbelt toward her. She removed the pistol from the holster. It was her father's gun, the one she had given Bolt.

She huddled against the wall, terrified. She couldn't bear to watch the men fight, and yet she couldn't take her eyes off of them. She flinched every time Jake landed a blow. She waved the pistol in the air, trying for a clear shot at Jake.

Jake lunged at Bolt. Bolt brought his foot up in the air. Jake tripped over the extended foot, landed flat on his face. Bolt rolled the drunken man over on his back. He used Jake's face for a punching bag. He banged him in the right eye, landed a blow to the left side. He smashed Jake's nose, flattening it.

Jake rose up, dumped Bolt on his ass. Jake seized the advantage. He sat on Bolt's chest, wrapped his large hands around Bolt's neck. He squeezed his Adam's apple. Bolt chopped at Jake's neck. Jake relaxed his choking hold. Bolt squirmed out from under.

Anita aimed the pistol at Jake, cocked the hammer back. But, the men were tangled again.

Bolt shot a hard right to Jake's face, caught him off guard. Jake bounced in the air, tumbled onto the bed. He hit at an angle. He tried to get off the soft feather bed, went the wrong way.

Anita saw him falling toward her. She thrust the pistol straight out in front of her. She closed her eyes and squeezed the trigger with both hands.

Jake took the bullet in the stomach. As he hit the floor two feet from Anita, she shot again. She emptied the pistol. Jake's arm flopped in the air, struck the carpetbag. It tipped over beside him.

Anita's money spilled out of the open satchel, landed beside Jake's face. Blood spurted from his wounds, stained through his shirt, his trouser leg. A pool of blood formed under his body, spread in a circular pattern.

Jake tried to get up. Couldn't. His head fell to the side. His eyes fluttered open. Three inches from his face was more money than he'd seen in his entire life. He stared at the money, saw the pool of blood spread out from under his shoulder, creep toward the scattered stacks of bills.

The bills stained crimson.

Blood.

Money.

Blood money.

So close.

So far away.

It was the last thought he ever had.

\* \* \* \* \* \* \* \* \* \*

Bolt dragged Jake's body outside and dumped it some distance from the house. He would let the sheriff take care of it in the morning. By the time he got back in the house, Anita had finished scrubbing the blood stains from the floor. She had removed the few stained bills from the bottom of the stack of money and set them to dry.

"Bolt, there's nothing left for me. Paul's gone. Papa's gone. I can't stay here at the ranch any more. There's no place for me to go."

"Don't you have any relatives or friends?"

"Papa and Paul were my life. And then I thought Jake would take care of me."

"Anita, life can be whatever you want it to be. I know you're sad about your father and Paul, and you should be, but life is for the living. You can brood the rest of your life about your bad luck. And be miserable. Or you can look for happiness and find it."

"That's easy to say."

"You can do whatever you want, Anita. Just decide what you want to do with your life, what will make you happy, then start making your plans."

"But I don't know what I want to do."

"You can't decide right now. But, think about it. Put the horror of Paul's death out of your mind. Remember Paul and your father in a good way. Accept the fact that Jake was a bad man. The Guthrie brothers, too. They're dead. They can't hurt you anymore."

"I know you're right, Bolt. But it'll take time."

"You'll be all right."

\* \* \* \* \* \* \* \* \* \*

Bolt helped Anita down from her horse. He unfastened the thongs on the saddlebags, flipped the leather flap back and removed Anita's satchel. Tucked safely inside was Anita's money, the bank draft. It was ten o'clock the next day.

Inside the bank, Bolt set the satchel on the counter in front of the teller's cage.

"Good morning, Miss Pike," said the banker.

"Good morning, Mr. Davis. I'd like to put my money back in the bank."

She could tell by the surprised expression on his face that Mr. Davis was curious, but she offered no explanation. He was a short man, fidgity. She opened the satchel and dumped the contents in front of the banker. Mr. Davis counted the money twice and then wrote out a record of deposit.

"Thank you," she said politely.

"Oh, by the way," said Davis, "there was a gentleman in here yesterday afternoon asking for your money. About closing time."

Anita's eyebrows shot up.

"What do you mean?"

"Jake Brady. Think that was his name. Said he was your husband. Said you'd taken ill and wanted him to pick up your money. I think he was drunk. Sure smelled like it. I told him you had picked it up the morning before. I hope I did right."

"You did fine, Mr. Davis."

She grabbed her satchel and stormed out of the bank. She held her temper until she reached her horse and then she exploded. Her face flushed with hatred.

"That dirty, low-down, sneaky no-count! Jake tried to get my money! And that pipsqueak, Mr. Davis. He had no right to tell Jake anything about my money. That's why Jake came out to the house last night. To get my money! Damn him!"

Bolt put his hands on her shoulder.

"Calm down. It's over with. Don't torture yourself anymore."

She looked up at him, searching his eyes. "You're always so calm, aren't you?"

"Not always," he grinned.

She took a deep sigh before she spoke again.

"I'll tell you what, Bolt. I'll buy you lunch today. I owe you."

"You don't owe me anything, but I accept."

"I've got some things to do right now. I want to look for a place to stay. A boarding house. And I have some other business to take care of. How about meeting me about noon? Delmonico's all right with you?"

"Fine. I have some things to do, too. I have to talk to the sheriff. Meet you at noon."

\* \* \* \* \* \* \* \* \* \*

It was a quarter past noon before she got to Delmonico's. Bolt was already there. He saw her come in the door, scan the room for him. He stuck a hand in the air, waved it until she spotted him.

"Sorry I'm late," she said. "It took me longer than I thought it would." She was beaming, her eyes glittering.

"No problem. You look a lot better."

"I'm so happy, Bolt. I found a place to stay. It's perfect. The people are so friendly and it's big. Two rooms."

"I'm glad for you, Anita."

"Will you help me move some of my things this afternoon?"

"Yeah. I'll get Tom to help us."

"Let's have champagne. It's a day to celebrate."

Anita chatted endlessly during the meal, telling Bolt that she wanted to do something important with her life. Maybe teach. She wanted to paint and study, play the piano. Most of all she wanted to marry a good man someday and raise a family.

"You're going to take on the whole world at once," he teased. He was glad to see her so enthusiastic. When they were through eating, she sat quietly until the dishes had been cleared from the table. Only their glasses and the half empty champagne bottle remained.

"I've saved the best news for last." She reached down to the purse in her lap, opened it and extracted a long white envelope, handed it to Bolt.

"What is it?"

"Open it and find out." Her eyes sparkled with joy.

Bolt opened the unsealed envelope, drew out the papers that were inside. He saw the large bold letters at the top: DEED.

"I don't understand."

"That's the deed to Papa's ranch. It's yours now. I had it transferred to your name. That's what took me so long."

"But. . . ."

"It includes the water rights."

"Anita, I can't accept this."

"Yes, you can. I want you to have it. I'm so grateful that you helped me understand myself better. I'm happy now. I know everything will be good. It makes me happy to give you the ranch. Don't take that away from me. It's my way of saying thanks."

"You don't need to thank me."

"Then just call it stud service," she grinned. "It was worth it."

\* \* \* \* \* \* \* \* \* \*

"What are you doing sleeping this time of day?" Bolt asked.

"Just resting," said Penrod. They were in Tom's room at the Dodge Hotel.

"I need a favor."

"Oh, no you don't."

"Nothing dangerous this time."

"I'll bet."

"Just need your muscles to help move Anita's things in to town. And I've got some good news."

"What's that?"

"We own ourselves a ranch."

"You're kidding."

"Nope. Anita signed over her deed to me."

Tom slapped his leg and laughed. "Sonofabitch! Now the women are paying you for services rendered. It must have been a good piece of ass."

"It was. Tom, you going to a whorehouse tonight?"

"Might."

"Might go with you."

Tom looked at him, surprised.

"You mean you're actually going to pay for a woman?"

"Nope. Just window shopping. I been thinkin' about buying me another brothel."

\* \* \* \* \* \* \* \* \* \*

Bolt and Tom spent most of the afternoon helping Anita load her few belongings in the buckboard. She took only her clothes and personal things, left the furniture and most of her possessions there.

When they were through packing, she gave them a tour of the ranch by horseback.

\* \* \* \* \* \* \* \* \* \*

It was early evening when Bolt and Tom left Anita at her place to visit the whorehouses.

"Which one do you want to go to?" asked Tom.

"Hell, you're the expert."

"There are plenty to choose from."

"I suppose you've tried them all."

"Not yet. Do you want a sleazy one, a fancy one? Expensive, cheap?"

"I want the best."

"Charlie's Palace."

"Lead the way."

Charlie's Palace was at the south end of town, tucked back two blocks from the main street. Like so many other such places, it was a combination hotel, saloon and brothel. When Bolt stepped inside, he knew it had class. A beautiful blonde, dressed in a shimmery gown, entertained the customers who sat at tables below the small stage. She sang ballads, her voice low and husky.

"Hello, sweetie," said a buxom brunette as soon as Bolt and Tom sat down at the bar. She pressed her warm body against Bolt's, tweaked his crotch. "You want to have a good time?"

"Not now, sweetie." Bolt smiled, accepting her brief kiss before she left to find a more eager customer.

"Hello, handsome."

The voice was deep, sensual. It belonged to a blonde whose large breasts jutted out of a red satin costume. She snuggled up to Tom, ran slender fingers around his body. She placed her hand on his thigh, wriggled her hips sensuously.

"How about a drink?" Tom asked her.

"Sure, honey."

Bolt ordered a drink for himself, leaned back and took in the atmosphere of the place. He wondered how much a place like this would cost. It was more plush than the whorehouse he owned in Abilene. He'd find the owner later and see if he was interested in selling. Now that he owned Anita's ranch, he might stick around Dodge City for a while.

When Tom went upstairs with the glitter gal, Bolt moved over to the tables in front of the stage. The tall girl on the stage was stripping out of her long red gown. Her body gyrated to the tune of the tinkling piano. Bolt watched until she finished her act and disappeared behind a curtain.

He leaned back in his chair, studied the structure of the building. High beams, sturdy posts. Carpeted spiral stairway.

The beautiful red haired girl coming down the spiral stairs caught his eye. Her shiny blue gown was tight, sexy.

Bolt's eyes widened.

He recognized the girl, couldn't believe it.

Sandra Jacobs walked down the stairs.

Little Sandra Wissner had grown up.

# CHAPTER TWENTY

Chad Fisher ran a hand through his greased-down hair, squinted his cold brown eyes.

"Damn it! Bolt's somewhere in this fucking town. Everybody we've talked to has seen him today."

"We've checked almost every place, except the whorehouses," said Will Atterbury.

"The desk clerk at the Dodge Hotel said he saw him leave a while ago with his friend Penrod," added Bob Steckley.

The three bounty hunters arrived in Dodge City shortly after noon, checked into a dumpy hotel at the edge of town.

The rest of the day had been a wild goose chase.

They followed every lead they got. They checked every restaurant, saloon and hotel in Dodge. They visited the bank, the barber shop, the stables.

By late afternoon, they split up. Steckley checked the Pike Ranch, found it empty. Fisher waited for over an hour at the Dodge Hotel for Bolt to show. Atterbury rode his horse up and down the main street, watching for the outlaw.

They stopped their search long enough to eat supper. It was dark when they finished.

"I'm going to find a poker game," said Fisher. "If I get lucky, Bolt will show up. That's one place he can't stay away from for very long. All I got to do is find out where the best poker games are. Bolt's got class. He'd go where the stakes are high."

Fisher's eyes were cold steel.

He hated the man they called Bolt.

He had a great respect for him, too. Bolt had been smart enough to outwit him twice before.

He wouldn't do it a third time.

\* \* \* \* \* \* \* \* \* \*

Chad didn't know how many times he had crossed Bolt's path that day, missing him by minutes or seconds.

Bolt didn't know either. He didn't know he was being stalked. Still.

\* \* \* \* \* \* \* \* \* \*

Sandra Jacobs came down the steps and walked toward the bar. She wiggled her sensuous body up against a cowhand seated at the bar. She leaned over, kissed him on the cheek. When she lifted her head, she saw Bolt watching her. She turned away quickly, ran for the stairs.

Bolt jumped up and followed her. She reached the top of the stairs, went into a small room and closed the door.

Bolt opened the door a minute later, went inside and slammed the door.

"Sandra, what in the hell are you doing in a whorehouse?"

"It's none of your business," she said defensively.

"It damn sure is! You don't belong here!"

"It's not what it looks like, Bolt. I'm not a . . . whore."

"What dya mean? This is a whorehouse, Sandra. Not a Sunday School class." She was right, of course. It was none of his business if she was a whore. But he felt betrayed, cheated. Jealous, too. But he didn't like the idea of little Sandra Wissner being pawed by drunken, sometimes cruel men.

She sat down on the edge of the bed, was about to cry.

"I was wrong, Bolt. I know that now."

"You lied to me, Sandra. You told me you were happily married. You sure don't act like it!"

"I didn't lie. I am married. I haven't done anything wrong yet. This is my first night here."

"Why? Why did you do it?" He walked over and sat beside her.

"I was just so lonesome without my husband. And then after you made love to me the other night . . . well, I just wanted more. I thought it would be exciting to work here for awhile. I was wrong. I got so scared when I saw all those filthy drunken men. I mingled with the crowd but I couldn't force myself to go through with it. My boss was watching me. He got mad. He jerked me around and told me I had to sleep with any man who had the money. I went upstairs to calm down and then came back to try again. That's when I saw you. I'm so ashamed."

"Nothing to be ashamed of. I'm glad you didn't go through with it. You're a beautiful woman. This could have ruined you forever. It could have steered you wrong. Most whores hate men. Did you know that?"

"No."

"If you need sex, there are better ways to get it. There are many decent men who would be good to you. You have a right to choose your friends."

"I want to leave, but I'm afraid of my boss."

"Come on. I'll take you home. There won't be any trouble."

Bolt took Sandra's hand, walked out of her room.

The door across the hall opened. Tom and the busty blonde stepped outside.

Tom saw Bolt and Sandra, smiled.

"Welcome to the club," Tom teased as he passed Bolt.

"Go to hell," Bolt muttered. "I'm leaving now. See you back at the hotel."

They rode double on Bolt's horse the few short blocks to her house. Bolt went in with her.

"What was your friend laughing about?" she said as she put a couple of logs in the fireplace. She lit the logs to take the chill off the house.

"A standing joke. Tom knows I don't buy the favors of young women. When he saw us coming down the stairs, he assumed I was a liar."

"Bolt, remember what you told me back there? About choosing a decent man if I wanted sex?"

"Yeah."

"Well, I choose you." She slithered against him with her warm sensual body.

\* \* \* \* \* \* \* \* \* \*

Bolt started back to his hotel, but he was restless. He and Sandra had made love. He was stimulated now, restless.

He needed a poker game he could get into. He'd been lucky so far today. Maybe his luck would hold.

He went to the Sundown House. That was supposed to be the best place in town to play poker. The stakes were high, but so was the quality of players.

He entered the saloon and headed for the bar. The place reeked of cigar smoke and whiskey. He'd watch the action for a while before he got into a game.

Bolt hadn't seen the two men sitting at a corner table.

Their hat brims were pulled down, partially covering their faces.

But, they saw him. Will Atterbury tipped his hat, a prearranged signal to Chad Fisher that the man who just entered was Bolt.

Chad would have known him anyway. Bolt had that special presence that Chad expected he would. Fisher was sitting at the bar, sipping a whiskey, three barstools from Bolt.

Bolt ordered a drink, studied the other men at the bar.

"Another whiskey," said the tall man three stools away.

"Here you go, Mr. Fisher," said Bill Benson, the thin, bald bartender as he served Chad.

"I hear this is a good place to play poker," said Fisher.

"Fair enough. You a good player?"

"Yeah, I'm good. Real good. Nice town, Dodge City."

"Good as any. Where you from?"

"Texas."

"You stayin' in Dodge long?"

"Who knows?"

Bolt listened to the banter between the two men. He studied the neatly dressed man who came from Texas. There was something about the tall man that grated against his nerves. His arrogance. His dark hair. The way it was all slicked down with grease. The man was neat enough, clean shaven, but he looked greasy to Bolt. He was smooth, too smooth to suit Bolt's likes. The way he bragged about his poker playing.

His eyes. That was another thing he didn't like about the man. His eyes were dark, cold as steel. Bolt figured the Texan could get real mean if he wanted to. Fisher, the bartender had called him. Name didn't ring a bell. If he was as good at poker as he claimed, seems he'd have heard of him.

Fisher downed his drink and clunked the empty glass on the bar top.

"Think I'll try my hand. See how you folks in Kansas play poker."

There were five players at the table Fisher headed for; one empty chair.

"Mind if I sit in?"

"Pull up a chair," said a wide-shouldered man in his early forties, wearing a Stetson with a Montana crunch. "Ante's a buck, playing five-ten. Hundred dollar buy-in."

"Thanks, gents," Fisher grinned. He bought a hundred dollars worth of chips. The bets were five dollars except for the last, when a man could bet ten. The owner allowed only one of these in his establishment and insisted on the hundred buy-in so that sharps or pikers couldn't weasel in for twenty and cause hard feelings. He wanted the players to enjoy the game.

There was a sign posted near the tables that the owner had put up: NEVER BET MORE THAN YOU CAN AFFORD TO LOSE.

Fisher played cautious at first. He won some pots, showed his hands. He tested them as much as they tested him. They called his every raise, his every hand. He didn't bluff.

One man dropped out, cashing in his original buy-in chips.

Fisher stepped up the play. The pots got bigger. The chips started flowing toward Fisher. His cold eyes didn't betray a single hand. His skill was formidable.

Bolt, looking on, grew interested. Very interested. He liked a challenge. Mr. Fisher was the best he'd seen in a while.

Bolt's hand started itching to get into the game. The swick-swick of cards, the clatter of chips, the swirl of tobacco smoke, the reflected glow of overhead lanterns with tin shades, the gleam of the green baize, all worked their hypnotic spell on his senses.

He strode over to the table.

"You could use a sixth," he said quietly.

"Set a cheer," said an old-timer who had managed to keep his head above water. "Maybe you can get them chips back in fair circulation. Fisher here's a mighty keen draw player."

Bolt clanked five double eagles together, shoved them toward the banker.

The banker counted out blues, reds and whites, scooted them across the table.

Fisher dealt the first hand. Bolt couldn't draw well enough to stay. He watched Fisher build up the pot, take it with kings full.

It took him ten minutes to read Fisher's play.

Every time the man caught, his right shoulder dropped slightly. It was almost unnoticeable. The other players studied Fisher's face for signs, but there were none. Just that right shoulder dropping.

Bolt began to win more often. The pots got bigger.

Two men dropped out, cleaned.

Two stayed, watching the pots go to Fisher, then to Bolt.

"You boys want to buck heads?" said the man wearing the pinched Stetson.

"Looks to me like they want to lift the limit," said the old-timer.

Bolt looked at Fisher. Fisher smiled.

"Suits me," said Fisher.

"You boys had enough?" Bolt asked.

They replied by scraping chairs, rising. The old-timer paid out the cash, shoved the cigar-box bank to Bolt.

"You take keer of the cash," he said. "I'm gonna go take me some poker lessons all over again."

"No limit?" Bolt asked Fisher.

"Ten dollar ante."

"Deal," said Bolt.

Fisher was hard to bluff, but Bolt took some hands when Fisher's shoulder didn't drop. It was getting easy. Too easy.

The pots swelled and a crowd gathered.

Bolt caught Fisher in a bluff. A murmur of approval from the lookers.

Fisher's chips began to dwindle.

Bolt dealt a hand. He studied his cards. Three aces, a king, a nine. Fisher opened with fifty dollars. Bolt bumped him. Fisher bumped back. Bolt raised a hundred. Fisher called.

Fisher took one card. Bolt took one.

He paired his kings.

It was time to go for it.

Fisher's right shoulder dropped. He bet two hundred.

Bolt raised another hundred.

Fisher raised it back.

Bolt raised it two hundred.

Fisher riffled his chips. He had three hundred or so left.

He called.

"Full house," Bolt said.

"Same here."

Bolt spread his cards out, aces over kings.

Fisher held queens over tens.

Bolt pulled in the pot.

"Tough luck," he said.

"More likely more than luck," Fisher said tightly.

The circle of onlookers, sensing trouble, stepped back from the table.

Out of the corner of his eye, Bolt saw a man heading toward the table. The crowd parted to let him through.

The man came up on his left side.

Bolt recognized him. He had seen him twice before.

It was the same man he saw in Abilene when he rescued Cassie. The same man he'd seen at the church in Ellsworth.

Will Atterbury.

A hush fell over the room.

Bolt was braced. He knew it.

He looked Fisher square in the eyes.

Fisher let a smile creep over his mouth.

Bolt knew who he was then. He had been playing poker with the man he'd thought had given up on him. The bounty hunter.

"Your given name Chad?" Bolt asked him.

"Chad Fisher's the name," Chad said as he drew his pistol.

Bolt outdrew him. He shot Chad, then ducked down quickly and whirled around. His second bullet caught Atterbury in the head. Blood spurted from the hole in the middle of Atterbury's forehead. He slumped to the floor, dead before he hit the ground.

Bolt walked over to Fisher, saw the man had been fatally wounded. Blood stained a circle on the man's chest.

Bolt glanced up just in time to see another man approaching. Bob Steckley.

Steckley's hand went for his holster.

Bolt's bullet caught him in the chest before Steckley's pistol cleared its holster. Steckley crumbled to the floor, blood spurting from his chest.

"How'd you know where I was?" Bolt asked the dying man.

"One of your whores. Wanda. Fisher tortured her. She told him." His voice trailed off as death took his body.

Bolt went back to Fisher, saw him gasping for breath.

"You dirty sonofabitch!" Bolt said.

"You got me," husked Fisher, "but they's others out there just as good. Judge Wilkins won't rest 'til you're dead. He'll send others. They'll figure you out better'n I did and brace you when your guard's down. I almost had you, Bolt."

"Yeah, Fisher, you almost did."

"How'd you get onto me?"

"The way you sat at the table. Your eyes."

"My eyes?"

"You never looked straight at me. Like you was hiding. I ain't never seen you before, but you had seen me. Man won't look at you direct is hiding something. Another reason, too."

"Yeah?"

"You had better hands than I did. Man lets me win, and money's on the table, I get mighty suspicious."

"How'd you know I could have won?"

Bolt smiled slow, his eyes piercing Chad's.

"I been second dealing you the past five hands. Giving you one hand better every damn time. Yet you let me buy the pots."

"Guess I wasn't as smart as I thought," Chad croaked. The end was almost there.

"You learn a lot playing poker. About men. About what's inside your self."

"I heard you was a straight player, Bolt."

"I am. In a straight game. This one was crooked from the time you sat down at the table. Man hunts other men for a living's no better'n a skunk. Thing my father used to talk about a lot."

"What?"

"He who lives by the gun, dies by the gun."

"I don't remember that in the Bible."

"Same thing, Fisher. In Bible days, they used swords. They still died. We use guns."

"Yeah?"

"Yeah. And we still die."

## THE END

## ADVENTURE FOR MEN

**THE SURVIVALIST #1: TOTAL WAR** (768, $2.25)
by Jerry Ahern
The first in the shocking series that follows the unrelenting search of ex-CIA covert operations officer John Thomas Rourke to locate his missing family—after the button is pressed, the missiles launched and the multi-megaton bombs unleashed . . .

**THEY CALL ME THE MERCENARY: THE KILLER GENESIS**
by Axel Kilgore (678, $2.25)
Hank Frost is blood-hunting his way through the jungles of Central Africa. And he's carrying his best equipment, along with a vicious vendetta—against a crazy rogue commander who massacred Frost's outfit to the very last man!

**THEY CALL ME THE MERCENARY #2: THE SLAUGHTER RUN**
by Axel Kilgore (719, $2.25)
Assassination in the Alps . . . Terrorism in the jungle . . . Deception in Washington. And Hank Frost is caught in the middle—with a nymphomaniac wife of a general by his side who'll have him as a lover . . . or have him dead.

**THEY CALL ME THE MERCENARY #3:**
**FOURTH REICH DEATH SQUAD** (753, $2.25)
by Axel Kilgore
After losing his prize charge to terrorist kidnappers, Hank has to gut his way through a sado-masochistic torture team, neo-Nazi gunmen and a vastly powerful Fourth Reich conspiracy to get him back. He finds help from a beautiful Mossad agent who's on his side—so she claims . . .

*Available wherever paperbacks are sold, or order direct from the Publisher. Send cover price plus 50¢ per copy for mailing and handling to Zebra Books, 475 Park Avenue South, New York, N.Y. 10016. DO NOT SEND CASH.*

## DON'T MISS THESE HEROIC FANTASY FAVORITES
## BY MIKE SIROTA

**RO-LAN #1: MASTER OF BORANGA** (616, $1.95)
Swept into a strange, other dimensional world, Ro-lan is forced to fight for his life and the woman he loves against man, beast, and the all-powerful evil dictator, the MASTER OF BORANGA.

**RO-LAN #2: THE SHROUDED WALLS OF BORANGA** (677, $1.95)
Love and loyalty drive fearless and dashing Ro-lan to return to the horrifying isle of Boranga. But even if he succeeds in finding and crossing through the warp again, could he hope to escape that evil place of strange and hostile creatures?

**RO-LAN #3: JOURNEY TO MESHARRA** (726, $2.25)
Pitted against a savage horde of Amazons, terrible sea creatures and a horrid bloodletting ceremony, Ro-lan and his faithful companions undertake a journey into the dominion of an ancient Mesharran—whose legendary powers may equal those of the Master of Boranga!

**THE TWENTIETH SON OF ORNON** (685, $1.95)
Dulok, the twentieth son of Ornon, is determined to become the Survivor—the sole ruler of the mighty kingdom of Shadzea. But he is also determined to avenge the death of his mother—whose blood was spilled by the great Ornon himself!

*Available wherever paperbacks are sold, or order direct from the Publisher. Send cover price plus 50¢ per copy for mailing and handling to Zebra Books, 475 Park Avenue South, New York, N.Y. 10016. DO NOT SEND CASH.*

# TROUBLE-SHOOTING WESTERNS

**AMBUSH RANGE** (696, $1.95)
by Don P. Jenison
When Buck Randall returns to Bear Valley for his Brother's funeral, he stumbles into a cache of rustled cattle and a violent feud between families. But will he stumble across the man who shot his brother—or will he have to search him out?

**THE BRONCBUSTER** (671, $1.95)
by Mick Clumpner
Ross Dunbar is a broncbuster out of work, but when he wanders onto A K Ranch he finds plenty of it—dodging four armed men looking for a stranger to pin a murder rap on!

**HARD TRAIL TO SANTA FE** (676, $1.95)
by Tom West
Glory, gold and adventure attracted hundreds to the new trading route opening to Santa Fe. But Red Blake joined for a darker reason: Somewhere in the great Taos slave market, he hoped to find his wife. . . .

**BLOOD ON THE RANGE** (686, $1.95)
by Owen G. Irons
After spending eighteen years in prison for a murder he didn't commit, Ford finally returned to his home town. With his true love lost and his father dead, he swelled with smoldering resentment and cried bloody revenge!

**GALLOWS GOLD** (687, $1.95)
by James Parrette
Money is always at the root of Charlie Morgan's mistakes—especially when he shoots a man in the back to get it and finds that the price the law puts on his head is not what he'd bargained for!

*Available wherever paperbacks are sold, or order direct from the Publisher. Send cover price plus 50¢ per copy for mailing and handling to Zebra Books, 475 Park Avenue South, New York, N.Y. 10016. DO NOT SEND CASH.*

## SPECTACULAR SERIES

**THE SGT. #1: DEATH TRAIN** (600, $2.25)
**by Gordon Davis**
The first in a new World War II series featuring the action-crammed exploits of the Sergeant, C.J. Mahoney, the big brawling career GI, the almost-perfect killing machine who, with a handful of *maquis*, steals an explosive laden train and heads for a fateful rendezvous in a tunnel of death.

**THE SGT. #2: HELL HARBOR—**
**THE BATTLE FOR CHERBOURG** (623, $2.25)
In the second of the new World War II series, tough son-of-a-gun Mahoney leaves a hospital bed to fulfill his assignment: he must break into an impregnable Nazi fortress and disarm the detonators that could blow Cherbourg Harbor—and himself—to doom.

**THE SGT. #3: BLOODY BUSH** (647, $2.25)
**by Gordon Davis**
In this third exciting episode, Sgt. C.J. Mahoney is put to his deadliest test when he's assigned to bail out the First Battalion in Normandy's savage Battle of the Hedgerows.